Money Kills

1

Bakul Kumar

A DI Barnes Thriller

ACKNOWLEDGEMENTS

I am grateful to Caroline Z for editing and Emmy Ellis of
Studioenp for Book cover.

All characters in this publication are fictitious and any resemblance to real persons, living or dead is purely coincidental.

A DI Barnes Trilogy

1

The alarm went off at 6:00 a.m. and Jonathan Webley got ready to take his border collie, Jess, for a morning walk. He went to the Lickey Hills, a country park ten miles southwest of Birmingham, every day before he left for work. Jonathan had kept several dogs over the years including his current companion, Jess, who gave him the joy of walking in the woods. The weather had turned mild over the last few days, but Jonathan ensured that he wore a jacket just in case a chill breeze hit him when he reached the heath. As soon as they entered the park, Jonathan let Jess off her lead. She ran around enjoying the newer smells left by her canine friends in various places. Jonathan admired the tall conifers planted either side of the path, Scots pines and Douglas firs towered over the footpath. He always carried a mobile phone in his pocket to capture images of interesting landscapes, but avoided using ear buds to listen to music, preferring instead to enjoy the birdsong and humming of insects.

After a ten-minute walk in the woods Jonathan heard a faint cry, he shouted, 'Jess, where are you?'

He did not get the usual response of Jess rushing back to him on command, so he called again, 'Jess.'

He strained to hear the faint cry of a dog and strode

towards the noise.

Jonathan was puzzled to find Jess crouched, whining in the undergrowth. He turned on his mobile to use the torchlight app and shone it around where Jess sat.

A body was lying, curled up and not moving.

It was a woman. He shouted, 'Miss, are you OK?'

As there was no response and Jess continued to whimper, Jonathan didn't like the look of it and called 999 on his phone and asked for the police.

It was 7:00 a.m. before a Police Community Support Officer turns up and asks him where the woman is and if she is alive.

Jonathan replies shakily, 'I couldn't decide if she was unconscious or deceased since she didn't respond to my calls.'

The PCSO shouts to obtain a response. He doesn't hear one either.

He turns to Jonathan; 'You stay, keep your hound on the lead and make certain you don't contaminate the area.'

The next to appear after a phone call from the PCSO is the duty police officer, Inspector Kevin Rudd, from the neighbouring Rubery police station. With the help of the PCSO, he secures the crime scene and rings the central police station in the Queensway area of the city of Birmingham. They inform him that the CID will turn up shortly.

In his professional life, Kevin Rudd had come across a lot of cases of dead bodies ranging from elderly people dying alone at home to the grisly scene of dismembered bodies following road traffic accidents. Kevin was well versed in the drill to secure the perimeter of a crime scene but had never had to do so in the tranquil Lickey Hills, normally a pleasant wooded area popular with walkers.

As Kevin is speaking to the PCSO, a motorcycle screeches to a halt kicking up a cloud of dust and gravel. He wonders how the vehicle had accessed this place which was intended for walkers and bicycles only. The engine is turned off and a character, still wearing a helmet, approaches him.

He shouts, 'Oi mate. You can't come here. This area is sealed.'

Ignoring him, the rider wanders towards the crime scene. Before he could shout again the figure removes the helmet to reveal the face of an attractive woman.

'Madam, it is illegal to ride a motorbike in the Lickeys and moreover this is a restricted area.'

Smiling, the woman presents Kevin with her warrant card, the proof of identity and authority carried by police officers in the UK. He reads the badge, which states that she is a detective inspector and her name is Nikki Barnes.

'I apologise for bringing the bike in and will move it soon.'

Kevin could well imagine the lithe body under the lightweight leather jacket, skinny jeans and comfortable, stylish Skechers shoes.

After speaking to Jonathan Webley, she dons plastic overshoes and walks towards the body. After making an initial assessment, she rings her boss, Superintendent Bob Newton.

Newton had been wide awake since 4:00 a.m. mulling over what had happened to his department, and policing in general in the country, since the budget cuts of twenty percent which were intended to streamline the workforce. It meant getting rid of a lot of police officers and not replacing the ones who had retired. He answers the phone, 'DI Barnes, I will send Detective Chief Inspector Andy Hill, but he is attending to another incident in Manchester at the moment, so please handle the situation until he joins you later.'

After making the phone call, Nikki walks towards the body and, for the first time, takes in the vast wooded area, the towering trees swaying in the light breeze, their spindly branches saying hello. She films the scene of the crime using a 360 degree approach for her personal use, knowing that this first hand information will enable her to pick up a lot of clues during the inquiry. She finds the body curled up in a foetal position, with hands and legs tied, the neat clothes appear to be untouched. Shining the torch on the face reveals a young woman of Chinese descent. There were no outward signs suggestive of a struggle. She recognises an ink stamp on the victim's hand, the emblem of "Devil's Den", the famous nightclub in Birmingham.

Next to show up is the divisional surgeon, Dr.Thomas Freeman, who after twenty-five years as a police surgeon had finally earned the title of divisional surgeon but sadly no extra payment to go with the promotion. Nikki introduces herself and takes him to the crime scene. He walks towards the body wearing overshoes, making sure he doesn't disturb the crime scene.

He examines the body, inserts a thermometer, records the temperature and, turning to Nikki, declares, 'This woman must have been dead between ten and fifteen hours.'

Nikki nods in acknowledgement, but being an old fashioned doctor, he thinks the detective is another "PC Plod" and asserts, 'Rigor mortis has not set in, which means she has been dead less than fifteen hours and the thermometer reads 88 degrees, a definite fall of ten degrees. I am sure they taught you this in the police academy, but as a refresher for you, the body cools on average 1 - 2 degrees every hour and the normal temperature is 98.6 degrees Fahrenheit.'

'Thank you, doctor, for recording the time of death. Are there any external signs of injuries?'

'There is a blunt contusion at the back of the head,

but I will be able to tell you more after the post mortem.'

As Nikki is about to say something, Dr. Freeman makes a joke, 'I hope you are not squeamish, inspector! Come to the mortuary within the pathology lab at the Countess Hospital. I will schedule the post-mortem for midday.'

Nikki nods, 'I'll be fine Dr Freeman.'

Next to arrive at the scene is the crime scene photographer who takes several pictures from various angles and a short film and then makes way for the Scene of Crime Officers. The SOCO team gathers forensic evidence including samples of blood, hair and footprints. One of the officers takes impressions of fingerprints from the body and from Jonathan Webley. They place the evidence into protective packaging to be sent away for forensic analysis.

Nikki watches Khalid Hussain, the chief SOCO officer, who has a reputation for strict prevention of contamination of crime scenes. She could hear him screaming at his team, 'Secure the perimeter much further out than the earlier one.'

She approaches him, 'Khalid, I'm sorry to be a nuisance.'

Khalid, a portly Asian gentleman of Pakistani origin in his 50s, turns to Nikki and snarls, 'What do you want detective?'

'I sensed there was a dog around the body, can you check if there is any fur other than from Mr Webley's dog here?'

'Are you telling me how to do my job?'

'No, Khalid, I'm requesting additional samples and trying to be helpful.'

'Please stop interfering with my investigation, inspector, otherwise I will report you to your commissioner! How do you know there was another dog, other than the one here?'

'I can sense it.'

'Oh, so you are some kind of super smeller?'

Nikki didn't want to reveal to him that she had unusual sensory discrimination in smell, touch or vision including synaesthesia, a phenomenon, in which stimulation of one sensory pathway leads to automatic, involuntary experiences in a second sensory or cognitive pathway.

She decides that further explanation is a lost cause and moves aside. Kevin Rudd, who is listening to this conversation, is annoyed by Khalid's harsh tone.

'Don't take any notice of that old codger, he's rude to everyone.'

Nikki shrugs, 'Thanks. I'm OK with it. Water off a

duck's back.' She wanders back towards her motorcycle.

Visibility had improved in the Lickey Hills so Kevin is able to take an appreciative look at Nikki's tall, willowy figure as she walks through the woodland. He is captivated by her dusky complexion and midnight black hair flowing over her shoulders. A pair of arched luxurious eyebrows look down on her sweeping eyelashes. Delicate ears frame her beautifully shaped nose. Her brightly coloured lipstick draws attention to her dazzling white teeth when she smiles. As she is putting on her riding gear, Kevin admires her sculpted figure and tapered waist.

Fully aware that Kevin is still scrutinising her, Nikki gives a wry smile, thinking to herself, let him enjoy! She sits astride her pride and joy, her Ducati motorbike. Its low seat makes it manageable in the city as she coasts along, despite the bumps and potholes. It cost 17K to buy this beautiful beast, but she feels it's worth every penny.

Nikki wonders why she doesn't visit this part of the city more often. In her teens, she used to come here with her friends and enjoyed walking in the 500-acre country park. She fondly remembers springtime when the area is covered with bluebells, wood anemones, foxgloves, stitchworts and buttercups. Her mother, although a busy doctor, was also a keen botanist and had taught Nikki to appreciate the wild flowers growing under the conifer plantations of Norway spruce, Scots pines and Douglas firs. When they roamed around the woodland towards Lickey Warren, they would admire the orange coloured coral fungus, birch and sweet chestnut trees.

She starts the engine, glances at Kevin, who is still admiring her, smiles and rides away.

3

By the time Nikki reached the Bristol Road at 7:45 a.m., traffic had already built up. Buses and trucks had slowed the traffic further on this road, which was already reduced to one lane as the other two were closed for construction of new bicycle lanes. The commuters were irritated by the cyclists who would play a dangerous game of dodgems, weaving in and out causing disruption. The motorists also played a similar trick by driving closer to the bicycle lane, preventing the cyclists from doing the dirty on them.

She needed to go home to freshen up and start her investigations. The distance from Devil's Den to the Countess Hospital was around four miles and Nikki could hurtle down there in ten minutes.

The journey to her studio apartment in Harborne should have taken 15 minutes, but knowing the speed limits and rush hour, it could double the journey time. She navigated along Bristol Road then moved into the university campus road, flew along Pritchatts Road and from there sailed past Somerset Road and Barlows Road only slowing down at High Street. From there she rode along Lordswood Road reaching her apartment, in Court Oak, in just twenty minutes. She could use these vital ten minutes.

Nikki had bought an apartment in Harborne, a middle-class suburb of Birmingham, after she returned from her tour of Afghanistan, a period of her life which she always avoided mentioning to people. Her mother, who believed in Feng Shui, ensured that the second floor flat had an uncluttered entrance. It had one bedroom and the open plan sitting room comprised of a dining table with two chairs, a top of the range Apple computer with a second monitor and a wireless printer. She had inherited an old record player from her mother along with LPs of Motown singers, Elvis Presley, The Carpenters, Tom Jones and Engelbert Humperdinck. One day she had an interesting conversation with Hamid, the sixteen-year-old son of her colleague, Ayesha, who visited her place and waxed lyrical about the mysteries of the retro record player. The apartment was pre-wired with an intruder alarm, but Nikki had upgraded it with a Wi-Fi connection to her smart phone. She had set up live camera recording in her house using smart cameras. The kitchen was modest with an induction hob and a microwave as most of the time Nikki preferred healthy dishes, like salads, and rarely cooked a meal. A remote control opened the apartment door and Nikki turned on BBC Radio 4 so that she could listen to the morning news and current affairs programme. It allowed her to absorb what was happening in the world with a different perspective. Some of the old presenters were cantankerous and tended to lean towards the left of centre of politics.

Nikki had no political affiliation and usually sat quietly when her friends argued about the plight of the country and the world.

After coming out of the shower she applied light make up: foundation, blusher, mascara, a neutral eye shadow, defining eye shadow and eye liner. Nikki was a trendsetter in her own way. She wore an eye catching outfit, a light coloured suit with a Hermes scarf and black crinkle effect ankle boots which would allow her to ride her bike or chase a suspect because of the flat heels, yet still look elegant.

She picked up her bag containing a 13 inch Mac Air along with a first aid kit which included epinephrine and naloxone, closed the apartment door, started the engine and the tyres screamed as Nikki's Ducati raced towards the city.

4

As Nikki began her journey towards her first stop, the Mailbox, followed by Devils Den, she wondered how her mother, Dr Madhuri Dixit-Barnes, was doing. No doubt she was already at her surgery in Sparkhill, a deprived inner city area, whose inhabitants were mainly of Pakistani or Somali origin. Madhuri was always an early bird at work, a habit developed years ago as a strategy to avoid the barbed comments of her partner, Neville Barnes, an investment banker. Madhuri and Neville had met in London while she was working as a junior doctor. For years she had endured his relentless criticism of her looks and work ethic, accusing her of not caring enough for their children, palming them off on their nanny, Keisha Belinfante, a tall attractive Jamaican woman. Nikki found out later that Madhuri had deeper reasons for being unable to face Neville - his nefarious activities in banking and many adulterous affairs.

Nikki wanted to concentrate on her job so she put aside her family matters and rode towards the Mail Box using a route, which tended to be busy, but the easiest to navigate. She continued past Gillhurst Road, turned right into Woodbourne Road and at the roundabout continued into Augustus Road, a beautiful part of the city with mature trees and grand houses. She continued her journey at 20 miles per hour, the new speed limit set by the National Highways to cut down on accidents in built

up areas, a decision which Nikki wholeheartedly
supported.

The traffic near the school became busy as she
approached the Botanical Gardens; "yummy mummies"
blocked the roads with their 4 wheel drive cars, dropping
their precious children as near as possible to the school
gates. She grumbled under her breath that these children
should be walking to school to reduce the ever-
increasing levels of childhood obesity. Whilst stuck in
traffic outside the Botanical gardens, Nikki fondly
recalled how her mother used to take her and Andrew
there during the spring and summer. She would give a
vivid description of each plant, telling them to also look
out for unusual plants like heliconia, plumbago,
bougainvillea, and cacti in flower during summer and
orchids, orange blossom and prickly pears during spring.
Nikki found out in later life that her mother's collection
of plant specimens, accumulated during her school days
in Mumbai, were still shown to students for reference
and education.

Finally, the traffic moved and at the Five Ways
roundabout she exited into Islington Row Middleway
and then into Suffolk Street, Queensway. Nikki
remembered how Islington Row had been mired in
trouble recently when a taxi driver, high on cocaine,
collided with other vehicles resulting in the tragic deaths

of seven people. Since then, cameras had been installed and police stopped taxi drivers at random for drug tests. Nikki was only too well aware that this crackdown stretched valuable police resources without necessarily reducing drug taking.

She arrived at Royal Mail Street in 15 minutes, parked her bike and walked to the Mail Box first before making her way to Devil's Den.

5

Birmingham's iconic Mailbox building has an interesting history. It was the site of the Royal Mail's largest mechanised letters and parcels sorting office in the country with a floor area of 20 acres. Years ago, in a school study tour, Nikki visited the tunnel which was constructed to link the Mailbox and New Street railway station. The tunnel allowed electric tractors hauling carts laden with sacks of mail to be driven from the station to the Mailbox.

Nikki exited the lift on the third floor, the location of BBC Midlands TV station. She had been invited to appear on the BBC Asian programme to speak about the alarming rise in gun crime and use of drugs in the city. On arrival she was intrigued to note that the open plan studio had colour-coded corridors with Birmingham street names for ease of identification. The programme assistant, Jas Narula, showed her around including the radio drama studio where the famous radio programme, The Archers, was recorded. It had sci-fi like, grey, padded foam walls allowing the characters to seem very far away when they are not. She admired the floor to ceiling windows of the TV studio which let in light and had breathtaking views of the canal areas outside. The interviewer, Harshal Bhogal, also known as "Harsh", was overawed by Nikki's presence, she could hear the producer prompting him from behind the screen. He asked her questions about the issues on gun crime, which she deftly answered with statistics to support her opinion. After the fifteen-minute interview, Harsh removed his earpiece, leaned forward expectantly and asked her out. Nikki smiled, firmly refused and left the studio.

Nikki walked down the steps behind the BBC studio, passed several smart restaurants which had not opened yet and looked across at the building called the "Cube" where she had, at one time, considered buying an apartment. They constructed the Cube from concrete, with two fireproof cores rising either side of the building. The glossy property developers' brochure included an interview with the Birmingham-born architect who managed the project. He explained that the design of the building evoked the city's industrial heritage and gushed about the cladding, which referenced the heavy industries of Birmingham, metal plate works and car plants. The crystalline interior was intended to echo the historical Jewellery Quarter of central Birmingham. Initially smitten by this modern city centre location, Nikki later decided that a one-bed room flat for around 250K in this swanky place did not really suit her, hence she opted for the pleasantly quirky, but affordable, apartment where she now lived.

She took a left turn at the Cube towards the canal side passing moored boats, pub beer gardens and roof terrace gardens. She reached the Malthouse Pub where the then US President Bill Clinton enjoyed a pint on the balcony during the 1998 G8 summit. Two doors away from the pub was Devil's Den. It was a mill in the past, now converted into an upmarket nightclub by the Romanian owner, Ionut Vasilescu, who was well known to the police. Ionut had amassed money by extortion, prostitution, drug dealing and money laundering through his club. Meanwhile, the authority of the police had been weakened by financial constraints, job cuts and low morale. Consequently, even some senior police officers felt powerless and resigned to the fact that turning a blind eye to a little bit of weed and a good time for youngsters was worth it to avoid the wrath of this powerful Birmingham criminal.

Nikki went to the back entrance of Devil's Den where she found Ivan Popescu, the bartender, clearing up the mess from the night before. She explained the reason why she was there and asked if she could watch the CCTV from last night.

Ivan took her to the security room, started the CCTV feed and when the image of the Chinese girl appeared, Nikki said, 'Do you remember this girl?'

'It was busy last night, I can't remember them all.'

'Come on, she was pretty. How could you miss her?'

'Come to think of it, yes she was pretty, but she was a lot of trouble!'

'What do you mean by that?'

'She came in alone and drank by herself until a handsome Indian bloke, with whom I think she was already acquainted, came and bought her the most expensive champagne.'

'OK, that's nothing. Boy meets girl.'

'No. When he began talking, she became furious and pushed him off of the chair.'

'Well?'

'It didn't stop there. She then gave him a cuddle and took him outside.'

'Interesting. How do you know all this when you said you were busy?'

'I'm a professional. I keep an eye everywhere and particularly on beautiful women who ask you to keep their champagne chilled till they come back.'

'Did they come back?'

'Yes, and they began drinking. A little later, a Chinese bloke arrived, spoke to the girl and then the fight started.'

'Who was fighting?'

'You can watch the video, it will become clear.'

Nikki saw a Chinese man in his mid twenties come up and speak to the girl and in a short while he and the twenty something Indian man argued and the brawl began. A minute later, she could see the club bouncer separating the two of them and the girl was gone.

Nikki asked Ivan to fast-forward the recording; the girl was nowhere to be seen. Ivan mentioned that the CCTV camera at the back of the club was not working and was being repaired, so there were no images of that area.

Nikki asked, 'Did the girl pay by card or cash?'

'Contactless.'

'What about the Indian man?'

'He paid by card, as the champagne was expensive.'

Nikki took the details of the man's till receipt and asked Ivan to pass her the card machine. She connected a USB cable from the machine to her laptop, entered a code and it loaded all the data from the machine onto the computer. She also took a copy of the CCTV footage.

As she was leaving, Nikki asked, 'Anything in particular which strikes you about this girl?'

'Yes, she seemed confident, beautiful and poised.'

'You were smitten then!'

'I don't know about that.'

'I may have to speak to you again. Can I have your details please?'

Nikki thanked Ivan, took another look around the club where the girl had been sitting, and where the fight took place and then left.

6

Nikki walked around outside the club looking for clues, since it had been dry last night she could not see any footprints. However, there was the unmistakable odour of a dog very similar to the one she had smelt in the Lickey Hills where the body was found. She continued to poke around, but her search came to a dead end.

She walked towards the Cube building and from there found the nearest cafe, asked for a tall latte and sat down.

After settling down in a quiet corner, her laptop came to life and she got to work. Nikki inserted a couple of codes and soon deciphered the card number of the Chinese girl who had paid by contactless transaction. Oh the marvels of hacking — thank you, Ayesha Begum, for being a specialist hacker and a great friend! It was she who had devised the programme that could give details of contactless card transactions.

She got most of the details of the Chinese girl just from her name and credit card details. Then she repeated the process for the Indian and Chinese men from their card numbers. It wasn't long before she had established an initial profile of all three characters using the credit card details and social networking sites.

Nikki raced her Ducati to the ultra modern Countess Hospital in the Dudley Road area. On her way, she passed Bath Row which was once the site of the iconic Birmingham Accident Hospital, famous for its trauma and burns unit. Although it closed in 2005, Nikki's mother said that in its heyday it was well ahead of its time and had laid the foundations of the current trauma service. After closure, this listed building became a part of the student accommodation complex.

The traffic slowed as she approached the Five Ways Roundabout, taking the third exit onto Ladywood Middleway. This area used to house the famous Birmingham Children's Hospital until it moved to its present site in Steely Lane. Nikki's mind once more wandered back to her mother's recollections of her early medical career as a junior doctor there.

Traffic was slow in Ladywood and it took Nikki another 5 minutes before she reached the Countess Hospital which now occupied the site of the old City Hospital. After parking her bike, she walked into the state of the art hospital building, admiring the glass walls which brought in abundant natural light. On arrival at the pathology department, she checked in with the receptionist. After she had been waiting for five minutes, Dr Freeman arrived in his theatre clothes.

'Good morning. Hope you found this place without difficulty.'

'Yes, doctor, it was easy to find and what a beautiful department you have.'

He asked her to change into greens and took Nikki into the recently commissioned, state of the art, autopsy room.

Dr Freeman sniffed disdainfully, 'Are you expecting gruesome dissection of body parts?'

'I'm prepared to watch to get the answers,' she replied with a deadpan expression.

He gazed at Nikki who radiated charm and self-assurance, yet did not entirely conceal an element of pain. Then he thought, let me get on with it, I'm not here to analyse her!

As they stand there, a table appears.

Dr Freeman makes firm and precise movements with the remote control pen in his hand.

Whilst Nikki is looking at him and the virtual autopsy table, he booms grandly, 'You've no doubt heard of it, but this is it in action.'

He continues, 'This virtual autopsy table allows me to explore the inside of a human body without disturbing the integrity of the actual body.'

Nikki nods.

'With its intuitive, gesture based interface, the virtual autopsy table changes the way we pathologists can interact with the data it produces. I can collaborate with multiple users and analyse complex data to gain a deeper understanding and insight into the functions and processes inside the body.'

Nikki was familiar with the use of artificial intelligence from her recent experience as a surgeon in Afghanistan. Pretending to be simply a good listener, she leaned forward in apparent concentration.

Freeman appreciated her body language, surmising that she could be a good listener.

Adjusting his glasses, he continues, 'I'm trying to dispense with invasive surgical procedures as it saves time and allows me to discover things which are difficult to find with traditional methods.'

'How many images does this table take?' Nikki maintains the deception of being a novice.

'For a detective, your attempt to grasp this technology is commendable. It scans the body using a computed tomography machine, creating 25,000 images of each section of the body.'

Freeman asks smugly, 'you know what a computed tomography is, right?'

'Yes, a lay person would refer to it as a CT scan.'

Pumping his fist in the air, he seemed to be mocking her with his gushing 'Well done!'

'I will analyse various parts of the body using this large touch sensitive LCD screen which stands like a table in an operating room, displaying an image of the body.'

He looks up at Nikki, checking that she remains attentive and resumes, 'With a swipe of a finger, I can remove layers of muscles, zoom in and out of the organs and slice through the tissues with a virtual knife.'

He looks around, hoping for a wider audience, alas, it is only Nikki, so he continues, 'Swedish police have used this technology in over 350 cases and it has been proved capable of detecting crucial and difficult-to-spot pieces of evidence, such as the angle of a bullet's trajectory, air pockets in the wrong place in the body and bone fractures in a burns victim.'

Nikki shuffles, continues to watch, but her gaze becomes glazed.

Freeman notices this change, but keeps quiet as he continues through the process. He explains that different tissues, bodily substances and foreign objects absorb the X Rays in varying amounts. He looks at the density value assigned to them by the software, which is then rendered into a 3-D visualisation of different colours and opacities. They show air pockets as blue, soft tissue as beige, blood vessels as red and bone as white.

After twenty minutes of visualising, Freeman stamps his foot on the marble floor, turns to Nikki and announces triumphantly, 'I have the answer. Someone murdered your victim with a single blunt trauma to the back of the head as can be seen by a single white opacity in the skull. I cannot see any other injuries. I have sent the bloods off for a toxicology screen.'

'What about other evidence?'

'I knew you would ask that. The victim had oral and vaginal sex before death. I have taken the specimens and sent them for DNA screening. You will get the answers by this afternoon along with the toxicology report.'

'Thank you, Dr Freeman, that was quite an interesting experience.'

'Are you sure? You are welcome to interact the next time there is a body!' and he winks.

'Thank you. I look forward to receiving the reports.'

She then sets off on the ten-minute ride to the Police Headquarters at Colemore Circus, Queensway.

7

Nikki checks in at Police Headquarters and takes the stairs to the fourth floor where she is met by her good friend, Ayesha Begum, the IT specialist.

'So, what have you been up to today?'

Nikki rolls her eyes, 'The usual post-mortem with that creepy, self-righteous Freeman, after following up some leads at Devil's Den.'

Ayesha gives an exaggerated wink, 'Did he show you his virtual autopsy table?'

'You are au fait with it then?'

'He sent me a text asking me to join him,' she answered with a glint in her eyes as she walked up the steps.

'Does he not realise that you could be his daughter's age, Ayesha?'

'Well!' Ayesha looks coyly at Nikki, 'What can I say. Love is blind!'

Nikki teases, 'You enjoy his attention my dear. He's obviously infatuated.'

They stop at the coffee machine on their way to the incident room.

Sipping her coffee, Nikki giggles, 'Freeman, may say to you, "Words cannot espresso how much you mean to me!"

Ayesha laughs at this feeble attempt at a joke. 'You and your silly one liners.' They head off to join the others in the open plan incident room to discuss their latest case.

It is 2:00 p.m. and at the head of the oval table in the incident room is DCI Andy Hill, flanked by Dr Freeman, Khalid Hussain, the Chief SOCO officer, his assistant, Harbans Kaur, data analyst from the HOLMES system, two more officers, detective constables whom Nikki didn't recognise, and Patrick Salt, the exhibits officer.

Nikki was familiar with the HOLMES system, an acronym for Home Office Large Major Enquiry System, created after the Yorkshire Ripper case in the 1980s. It manages huge amounts of data such as DNA, fingerprints, physical descriptions and offender profiles which is shared with other police forces across the country. Harbans Kaur was superb at her job, legend had it that she could retrieve data in nanoseconds. After years of experience on the beat, she reinvented herself as a computer buff and had been on active duty for a total of over thirty years. However, Nikki felt that Ayesha had more up to date IT skills and appreciated her adeptness in getting in and out of any system in no time, without a trace.

DCI Hill, a rotund man with stained teeth, addressed the meeting in his thick Brummie accent. Some ungenerous souls might associate the local sing song twang with a lack of intelligence, but Nikki had come to appreciate the warmth of the local people. To her ear the Birmingham accent was now familiar, but she still found the Black Country dialect impenetrable. At the police station, true yam yams - a term derived from their habit of using y'am for you are- would be heard greeting each other with 'Yow oroit, bab?', taking their leave with 'ta-ra a bit' or using obscure phrases such as, 'this ain't gettin' the babby a new frock and pinny' - an expression of frustration when an investigation was leading nowhere. Over the years, Caribbean and Asian influences added to the mix.

DCI Hill invited everyone around the table to introduce themselves. The first newcomer to his left was Detective Constable John Williamson, fresh from Hendon Police Academy, followed by Nina Kowalski, a criminal psychologist.

Hill interjects, 'Williamson might be a rookie, but he has a strong pedigree. His father was my mentor and a great investigator who left an impressive legacy of crime solving and we follow that tradition.'

Nikki clicked that John's mother, Anna Williamson, is the sitting Member of Parliament for the Harborne ward and the Home Secretary, number two in the British government.

Anna Williamson is known to be in favour of strict punishments and is also a staunch supporter of the "stop and search" policy which allows police to question an individual if they suspect that they are carrying a weapon, illegal drugs, stolen property or something which could be used to commit a crime. This had not gone down well with liberal analysts who feel that young black men are unfairly targeted, being more likely to be stopped and searched by police than white men. Successive governments, and the present Home Secretary, have ensured that "stop and search" is used as a vital policing tool, emphasising that nobody should be stopped because of their race or ethnicity.

During the introductions, other members of the police team gather. Each officer has a distinct role, an inside sergeant who collects all the data coming into the station regarding the case, an outside sergeant responsible for assigning police officers to take statements from the public in door to door enquiries, an exhibits officer who logs all items such as the victim's clothing, purse and phone and stores them after they have been examined. Additionally, a CCTV analyst who analyses all the data collected in the vicinity of the crime and the Officer in the Case who builds up a timeline and runs the case along with the DCI.

Once the introductions are over, DCI Hill turns to Nikki, 'DI Barnes, what have you got for us?'

Nikki moves towards the crime scene board and with a deadpan expression kicks-off, 'The victim is Mei Wang, a 19-year-old woman from Hong Kong and a Miss Hong Kong finalist. She's a student at the nearby Metro University, in her first year, studying medicine. She lives in a student accommodation block in Rubery close to her campus.'

Nikki pauses and looks around for comments.

Hill asks, 'Last known whereabouts?'

'She had a stamp on her hand from Devil's Den, the famous night club near the Mail Box.'

Ayesha looks up. 'So what did you find there?'

'She was seen drinking on her own, then with a good looking Indian guy.' She pauses and starts a video clip of the club's CCTV footage from her smartphone which relays the images to the screen.

'I met the bartender who was serving last night. He has an eye for attractive women so recalls seeing Mei. He corroborates what we see here on the video. She is drinking alone, and then an Indian guy in his mid twenties comes in and buys her expensive champagne. They drink, go out for a short while and come back.'

Hill asks, 'I can see that, what did the bartender think?'

'He had no idea where Mei Wang and the Indian guy

went to, they simply told him to look after the champagne bottle.'

'OK, continue.'

'As they drank, a Chinese gentleman in his late twenties or thirties walks towards them and after a couple of minutes argues with Mei.'

'So what then?' interjects Williamson.

'An altercation follows between the Indian and the Chinese guy. The bouncers come over, separate the two guys and at this point Mei disappears from the club.'

'So where did she go?' Hill asks.

'No idea. The CCTV at the back of the club was not working according to Ivan Popescu, the bartender.'

'Do you suspect this man?'

'Oh, the bartender? You can tell he likes young beautiful women. It's worth questioning him again.'

'What about the identity of the two men?'

'The Indian guy is Dinesh Malhotra, a 21-year-old, studying engineering at Metro University.'

Williamson leans forward, 'How do you think these two people met? He's an engineering student and she was studying medicine.'

'Metro University was established by the private

sector, 80% of its students come from abroad and 20% from within the UK. The campus is massive. It was built on what was formerly a golf course on the outskirts of Birmingham.'

Williamson muses aloud, 'Surely it's unlikely that they would have met on a huge campus like that?'

'It's worth finding out later. OK, any names for this Chinese guy?' Hill asked.

Nikki volunteers, 'Jian Li, son of Han Li.'

'You mean the local link for the Hong Kong Triad?'

'Yes, sir. That's him.'

'OK, we'll have to talk to these guys. What about your findings Dr Freeman?'

Freeman, who is wearing a pin stripe suit and bow tie, stands up and looks over at John, 'Welcome to the fold, son. Like the DCI, I worked with your father for many years and I hope you will continue the same tradition,' then turning around to the rest of the team, 'Sorry, it was a bit emotional to see John sitting there' and carries on, 'Mei Wang was 154 cm tall, weighed 48 kilos. She had one external injury at the back of the head.'

'A blunt injury then?' Hill asks.

'Yes, one fatal blow, but she also had a needle mark

between her big toe and the first one in the right foot. This corresponded to high levels of heroin in the blood, not enough to kill, but she would certainly have been high. There was no sign of a struggle and her nails were clean.'

'Anything else?'

'Yes, she had sexual intercourse with two individuals that day.'

'And how did you come to that conclusion Tom?'

Dr Freeman raises his eyebrows, grimaces, puts his hands on the table and grunts, 'I might be getting old, Andy, but I know how to deduce these things.'

'Sorry Tom, was just joking.'

'OK. I did a gross microscopic analysis of sperm found in her mouth and the vagina. I confirmed that they came from two different sources and as we speak DNA analysis is being carried out on those specimens in our laboratory.'

'What about her clothing and belongings?'

'Her clothing was untouched. There were no fibres on her clothes. Interestingly, there was another lingering odour other than her perfume.'

Nikki raises her hand, 'Was it the musky odour of an unwashed person?'

'Yes, strangely enough, true.'

Hill looks at Khalid Hussain, the SOCO officer, who adds, 'We found partial foot prints of a size 11 shoe with markings which suggest that the perpetrator was carrying something heavy.'

'Could that be caused by carrying a body?'

'Possibly, Sir. We were able to trace these prints for a few metres and then they disappeared into the brambles of a wooded area.'

'Is it possible that this thicket leads to Twatling Road or Warren Lane?'

'It's more towards Warren Lane.'

Looking at the team, Hill slaps the table decisively, 'Right, we need door-to-door enquiries and a meticulous search of where the victim lived, get CCTV coverage around her accommodation and the campus. Make sure we do a simultaneous thorough search around Warren Lane, Rose Hill, Monument Lane and question residents of the area including the Lickey Church and the local youth centre.

Khalid grins at Nikki, 'Inspector, we tested the turd near the body.'

Hill raises his eyebrows and snaps, 'What is this turd business? Some sort of joke, Khalid?'

'No, Andy. DI Barnes persuaded me to look at the faeces found near the body.'

'And?'

'It belongs to a dog, probably deposited an hour or so after the death of the victim.'

'Could it be that the dog followed the perpetrator?'

Nikki chips in, 'Guv, my hunch is that the dog belongs to the perpetrator, and it relieved itself at the site.'

Ayesha pipes up, 'Khalid, is it possible to undertake a DNA test to determine the breed of dog?'

Khalid looks bemused, 'Yes, we have a tool kit and we can undertake that task if the DCI wishes.'

Hill responds to the pleading look in Nikki's eyes and turns to Khalid, 'Do the DNA test and also analyse the faeces, please.'

'Thank you, Khalid, and I will check with the witness if his dog relieved itself at the site and what type of food it eats,' Nikki offers.

As the meeting is being adjourned, Hill takes Nikki aside, 'You have a new partner.'

'Why? Who?'

'John Williamson.'

'Guv, you know I like to work alone.'

'I know that, but John needs a good mentor, who better than you?'

'I don't have a car.'

John pipes up, 'If it's OK by you, DI Barnes, I'm a good driver with a roadworthy car.'

Ayesha mutters under her breath, 'Maserati I presume.'

John, quick on his feet, puts her straight. 'Not for me. I have a four wheel drive Subaru XV.'

'That's still a souped up sports car for boy racers.'

'Actually, it's a very unassuming car and I love it.'

Nikki brings the conversation to an end, looking at Ayesha, 'OK, John, see you later.'

John messages his dad.

"Need to know about DI Nikki Barnes. Been paired up with her. Give me a heads up."

8

Ayesha turns her attention to Nikki as John leaves the room.

'How do you feel about working with John?'

'You know what I am and who I am. I'm a loner!'

'Yes, I know, but Hill doesn't get that. Give it a go, try working with him.'

'Ayesha, we grew up together and you know damn well my quirks, habits.'

'How are your fits now?'

'Well controlled.'

'What do you mean?'

'Anxiety is a big trigger, I get an aura and if I can't control it, I end up on the floor with a fit.'

As she is talking, Nikki reaches into her handbag, takes out a hip flask and surreptitiously sips a few drops.

Ayesha is amazed that just a nip from the pocket flask restores Nikki to normality.

She quizzes Nikki, 'How are the supplies?'

'You mean my cannabis oil? Don't be shy about asking direct questions. I have a regular supplier.'

'Where does he get it from?'

'I don't ask questions, Ayesha. I make a request and he delivers.'

'You mean home delivery?'

'Yes, home delivery and no, he won't leave it with my neighbours if I'm not at home,' she chuckles.

'Is it still effective?'

'Yes, it works. I can't ask my doctor for a prescription.'

'Why not?'

'Are you mad? A prescription for cannabis oil would trigger an alert to the Home Office, which means I would be sacked.'

'Isn't it a good idea to be honest about your situation with the HR department?'

'What? And end my career?'

'You always believed in telling and upholding the truth. Why not now?'

'Good grief girl, you still play the dumb card sometimes and you aren't even a blonde!'

They both laugh at the silly joke.

'Nikki, you need to do something about working

with John.'

'I know. I need to sort myself out.'

'See you later.'

' Love to your little boy, Hamid.'

'He isn't little anymore. He's 16 years old now and already wants to be like me!'

'What married, divorced?'

'No, silly. An expert in coding. It absorbs all his spare time and energy.'

'That is better than going out and playing truant.'

'We have to thank Allah for small mercies.'

'Give yourself some credit.'

'OK. Got your point. Must dash. Bye.'

9

John Williamson finishes his first day at work and rings his girl friend, Tina.

There is the click of an answerphone,

'Hi, this is Tina, the budding journalist. I can't take your call right now. If you have a juicy story, please leave a message and I'll come back to you as soon as possible.'

John leaves a message:

'Hey, my gorgeous Journalist of the Year. I'm on my way home. Do you want me to get us a Chinese takeaway?'

As he uses his remote key to open the car door a message arrives.

"Son. I looked at info on DI Barnes. Lot of redacted memos. Will send mail. Summary - dangerous, ex army, ex doctor, can kill."

John a tall, slim, neatly dressed young man always wore understated clothing, avoiding expensive brand labels in an attempt to deflect attention away from his wealthy background. His mother had inherited a fortune from her diamond dealer father; she chose a career in politics and rapidly climbed the ladder to become the present Home Secretary. His father, Peter Williamson, had taught him to live a simple life and not to get carried away by splashing around his mother's wealth. Loosening his silk tie, given by his mother as a present to wear on his first day as a detective constable, he starts the engine.

He drives out of the car park and heads towards Monkspath, a large posh housing estate in Solihull, and the most affluent town of the region outside London. A survey of Quality of Life Index in 2013 named Solihull as "the best place to live in the United Kingdom." He had moved away from his parent's house, an eight-bedroom mansion set in five acres of land with animals in the highly desirable village of Hampton in Arden.

It baffled John why people would pay such extortionate property prices for the sprawling houses and gardens in Hampton in Arden. A small four-bedroom house would cost £600 K and the bigger ones, one million and the rest!

He was content to have found a nice three bedroom, semi-detached house in Monkspath for £400 K. His parents insisted on helping him out with the deposit for the house, but let him pay the mortgage. They never interfered with his daily life.

The 10-mile drive to his house should take just 35 minutes, but in the rush hour he could be stuck in traffic for an hour or more. As he passes Snow Hill Queensway and on to St Chad's Queensway, it brings to mind how the city of Birmingham and its surroundings had radically changed after the Second World War. Herbert Manzoni, the then city engineer and surveyor, believed that the answer to city centre congestion was to build a ring road on St Chad's Queensway consisting of a series of main roads linked by flyovers and tunnels, confirming his view that "the car is king". Little did he know that in the 21st century it would be a scene of chaos, traffic jams and air pollution?

At last the traffic begins to move along Belgrave Middleway and he passes the iconic Birmingham Central Mosque, built in 1969. Although clogged with traffic now, unbelievably these streets were once the scenes of high-speed motor racing. He remembered his dad telling him about the Birmingham Superprix, a motor racing meeting that was held regularly between 1986 and 1990. At that time, his father was a detective constable and witnessed first hand how the cars were thrown around the bumpy streets and hurtled down Belgrave Middleway. One year, torrential downpours from the tail end of Hurricane Charley drenched the circuit leading to several horrific crashes. Miraculously, the nearby Birmingham Accident Hospital handled the multiple accident victims without any fatalities.

The car edges south through the traffic onto Wake Green Road, Moseley, an area mentioned in the Doomsday Book of 1086 and famous for its 14th century St. Mary's Church.

In the past, John would often enjoy a walk around Moseley village with his parents, passing through some affluent areas cheek by jowl with social housing and rented accommodation.

In the 1990s, when his family regularly visited Moseley for a curry, his dad used to say to his mum, 'Did you know Nick Rhodes of Duran Duran was born here and his dad had a toy shop in the village?'

'Oh, Peter,' groaned his mother, rolling her eyes, 'How many times are you going to tell me that story about Duran Duran?'

His dad would always reply innocently, 'Did I mention that before, darling?'

The traffic gradually crawls towards Robin Hood Island, which has no connection with the legend, but is simply a misreading of "Robin Wood". Ten minutes away from home, he speed dials the local Chinese and orders the regular meal for two.

No sign of Tina yet.

10

John sets himself up with a can of lager and admires his own creation - his home.

He designed the interior of the house himself before meeting Tina. The walls were decorated in pastel shades; a three seater and a two-seater sofa adorned the living room with a small coffee table in the middle.

John had a preference for the open plan minimalist interior style. He had deliberately kept the living area furnishing to a bare minimum and ensured that the dining area was also uncluttered, hence two chairs and a table from IKEA occupied the space. The kitchen diner combined stylish functionality with free flowing space incorporating all the necessary kitchen appliances and induction hob without sacrificing clean lines and ease of movement. After meeting Tina, he allowed himself the luxury of two stools at the breakfast bar, where they could sit in the morning before they went off to work.

Tina and John became engaged after a whirlwind romance. She had her own apartment in Warley, west Birmingham and preferred to remain independent until they were married. However she allowed herself a token presence in John's house with a toothbrush, lingerie and pyjamas.

John's mind was flooded by thoughts of Tina and now a new arrival in his life - DI Nikki Barnes. What should he make of his dad's message - "can kill"? Did he mean that she is an out of control psychopath or someone planted by the intelligence services to annihilate undesirables? Does she kill with a knife or bare hands? Is she armed? Or could she be akin to the Lisbeth Salander character from Stieg Larsson novels, a sociopath, with her own guiding moral principles?

His train of thought is broken when Tina enters the house, 'Hello, darling. I'm home and I'm famished! Shall we eat?'

'And hello to you too! Yes, I'm fine, darling. The food is ready.'

'Don't need to be so sarky!'

He gives Tina a hug and stroking her hair whispers, 'Sorry, darling. Didn't mean to be rude.'

Returning his embrace, Tina plants a kiss on his forehead, 'Sorry to be insensitive. I've had such a long day, and I'm knackered.'

He pours a glass of Australian Chardonnay bought from the local supermarket.

Sipping her wine, Tina purrs in her sultry voice, 'So, tell me, how was your first day?'

As John begins to speak, he gets the impression that

Tina has already switched off and is just tucking into her food. He wants to explore his sneaking suspicion by saying, 'Yeah, and I farted loudly in front of the DCI.'

By this time, Tina is fiddling with her phone and without even looking up mumbles, 'Oh, that's great honey!'

John fumes, 'You didn't hear one word. You and your sodding phone!' and throws his food into the bin.

'I was trying to catch up with my messages and was listening to you. We women can multi task, John.'

'You were more interested in the phone than hearing about my first day.'

'I'm sorry,' wrapping her body around John, with lips quivering, 'I'll concentrate solely on you now, my darling.'

'Never mind,' he dismisses her concern, rubbing his eyes.

'Stop rubbing your eyes!' Tina slaps his hands.

'Since when did you become my mother?'

With pursed lips, she mutters, 'Since your mother abandoned you.'

John buries his face in his hands, 'Please don't go there.'

'Well, get off my back then!'

'Can we call it quits, please? I'm tired,' he slouches down in the chair.

'OK.' Tina puts the carton of takeaway food in the bin.

'It's your sodding phone going off again!' yells John.

Tina, who is brushing her teeth, comes running out and picks up the phone, 'Yes, I'll call you soon.'

'Who is that?'

'Work!' retorts Tina.

'But you've just come back from work', snaps John, arms folded across his chest.

'I'm a journalist.' Tina responds stiffly, 'My news is dynamic, not stale like yours John.' She gives an exasperated sigh.

This time there is a series of text messages accompanied by a variety of notification sounds. John, a classical music buff, notices one of them is a romantic Chopin message notification alert.

Tina moves away from John to the kitchen area, 'I need to take this.'

She types messages.

John is resigned to the thought that he has lost her to her passion, journalism.

At last they settle down together to watch a recorded Grand Prix, but, predictably, a few minutes later John notices that Tina is once more engrossed in her phone!

11

It's 8:00 a.m. and John arrives in the office, presuming that he would be the first to arrive. However, DI Barnes along with Ayesha is already in the office discussing the case.

'Good morning. Didn't you go home last night ladies?' John asks with a twinkle in his eye, pulling up a chair.

'Why? Are you implying that the atmosphere is a bit ripe?' retorts Ayesha.

John is flustered. 'No. Obviously I didn't mean it that way.'

Nikki defuses the tension, 'We arrived half an hour ago.'

'Any developments?' enquires John.

'Not yet. We were working on some assumptions, like how she was moved from Devil's Den to the Lickeys. There are no signs of forced interference although she must have had consensual sex.'

'Could it be that the victim was carried on the assailant's shoulder?'

'Yes. It's possible, as we discussed yesterday.'

Ayesha interjects, 'I didn't find any useful CCTV in the Lickeys or from the front of any houses on Rose

Hill.'

Nikki sighs, 'It's gonna be a long day, John, hope you had your porridge!'

'Yep, I've had my porridge, a coffee and I'm raring to go. My car is ready.'

'OK. John, let's go.'

'Where to ma'am?'

'We're going to some newly built flats called Horizon View in Rubery, where Mei Wang lived.'

'From there?'

'We'll see. By the way, when no one is around, call me Nikki. I don't like titles!'

'OK, ma'am!' and he laughs.

It takes forty minutes to reach Horizon View, a development of purpose built modern flats for students with an in house swimming pool, tennis court, gymnasium and a cafe. She ponders how much it must cost parents to fund their kids in this type of accommodation.

John echoes her unspoken thoughts, 'Must cost at least 1,500 to 2,000 pounds per month to live on this site.'

'Yes, but the students who come here are from

affluent families. They can afford these prices.'

John tries not to gape at the young women emerging from the gym attired in revealing, expensive, branded sports gear, he stutters in appreciation, 'Wow.'

Not one for distraction, Nikki chides, 'Come on, John. We need to get started.'

As she is walking towards the warden's office, Nikki can't help but compare this privileged lifestyle with that of the students she knows in the nearby Selly Oak area. There it's commonplace to find youngsters living in disgusting conditions with no heating, rising damp, leaky roofs, the victims of unscrupulous, greedy landlords.

Having donned surgical gloves, they use the key card to open the door to Mei Wang's flat. It opens to reveal a pleasantly decorated room with a large bed, study area, a kitchen diner and bathroom.

'Have you noticed that the laptop and iPhone are missing, but their chargers are still in the sockets? She was obviously not planning on going away.'

John looks around, 'The flat looks clean, no signs of disturbance. Everything seems to be in place. If someone was searching, they were thorough and left no signs of a break in.'

'I agree. Look,' Nikki wrinkles her nose, 'a used condom in the toilet.'

She examines medicines from the bathroom cabinet and shows them to John.

'What are these? Clozapine, Risperidone?'

'They're antipsychotic drugs used to treat schizophrenia.'

'I'm surprised that they'd allow a person with a history of psychotic illness to join medical school.'

'Oh yes, it's not necessarily a bar to becoming a doctor.'

'Seriously?'

'Unfortunately, with each relapse the brain function diminishes in the prefrontal cortex which is the area of higher executive functioning.'

'That's worrying, putting our lives in their hands.'

'Look, John, famous people like John Nash the mathematician and Rufus May, the Nobel Prize winning British clinical psychologist and several others have lived a successful life, and they were schizophrenic.'

'But they're not medical doctors!'

Nikki refuses to be drawn further and shuts down the topic, 'Let's call the SOCO team.'

A painstaking search of the flat reveals nothing until Nikki stumbles across a small hole in the wall concealing a camera facing the bed. She points it out to John who searches for similar devices and finds one in the wall opposite the sofa and another in the toilet.

Nikki closely examines the devices. 'This looks like a sophisticated camera system with a button somewhere to trigger it or it could even be voice activated.'

'How do you know all this Guv?'

'Wasted youth!' Nikki replies flippantly, tucking a stray lock of hair behind her ear.

'No,' John probes, 'you're being modest. The technology looks advanced, you must have been trained in this type of work.'

But Nikki brushes off his suggestion with a shrug, 'You learn on the job and also undertake research to learn about advances in technology.'

He rubs the back of his neck and chuckles, 'Perhaps, I should learn from you, boss!'

Nikki gives a wry grin, 'Come on. Let's speak to people in the gym and canteen in the basement.'

Nikki recognises a girl from Mei Wang's social media page: Jenny Craddock, a second-year medical student. The slender girl, kitted out in pink lycra shorts, is working hard on the exercise bike, her long legs pumping hard and tangled blond ponytail flicking from side to side.

'Hi, I'm DI Barnes and this is DC Williamson. Can we have a word with you Miss Craddock?'

Jenny stiffens, 'What do you want from me? I've done nothing.'

'Relax, Miss Craddock. We want to ask you about Mei Wang.'

'She's in the year below me and we hang out sometimes,' Jenny stutters.

Adjusting the lapels of his jacket, John asks, 'When was the last time you saw Mae?'

'Not in the last two days.'

Nikki notes the suspicion in Jenny's sharp blue eyes, she walks towards the bike and touching the handle says, 'Good workout today,' looking at the screen, 'One hour, 500 calories spent. Wow!'

Jenny visibly begins to breathe more easily and murmurs, 'What do you want to know?'

'Do you know who Mei goes out with? Her boyfriend or boyfriends?'

'Mei is a private person. I go out with her to bars.'

'Boyfriends?'

Jenny hesitates, 'Well. She has a couple. An Indian guy called Dinesh, he's an engineering student, and Jian

Li.'

'Is Jian Li a student too?'

'No. He works with his father.'

OK. What about Dinesh?'

'Dinesh is a nice bloke. He loves her...' she pauses.

'Yes, go on.'

John interrupts, 'And Mei, didn't feel the same?'

'You're right. She just wants a good time, although she likes Dinesh, he's very handsome.'

Then, as John's words sink in, Jenny clenches her fist and yells, 'What do you mean, "didn't feel the same" - past tense?'

'Jenny, I'm afraid Mei's body was found yesterday, in the Lickeys.'

Heavy teardrops roll down Jenny's cheeks, her slight body is wracked with sobs. She can barely get out the words, 'What happened?'

'We don't know yet. We're piecing together the information about her life.'

After a pause, John asks gently, 'Anything you can tell us about Mei or her boyfriends would be really helpful.'

Jenny smears the tears across her face with the back of her hand, but more tears fall anyway. 'Mei, had a taste for expensive clothes and a social life which Dinesh couldn't afford.'

'So, Jian Li fitted in?'

Jenny sniffs ruefully, 'Yes. Mei believed in getting the best of both worlds. She had Dinesh for sex and Jian to spend money on her.'

'So was Mei happy with both or did she have a particular preference?'

Jenny looks up though her tears, stunned, 'How do you know this?'

'Just guessing.'

'OK.' Jenny looks away as more tears well up, 'So she tried to keep Dinesh happy, but Jian could demand sex from her at anytime.'

'In return for money?'

'I wouldn't put it that way, but yes, he bought whatever she wanted.'

'Did Dinesh buy anything?'

'No. He got jealous of the growing relationship between Mei and Jian.'

'Did Mei tell you anything more?'

By this time Jenny begins to calm down, she sinks down on a stool, wiping her wet face, 'Dinesh wanted Mei to meet his parents as he was in love with her.'

John smirks, 'That was serious!'

'Yes,' pointedly avoiding him and looking at Nikki she continues, 'Mei avoided it and tried to tell Jian who threatened Dinesh a few days ago.'

'It makes sense,' John whispers.

'What makes sense?' yells Jenny.

'Nothing, Jenny,' reassures Nikki, holding her hand.

'You're holding back,' Jenny wails, 'you can't stop now. She was my best friend.'

'OK. We saw a video clip from Devil's Den bar. It showed Dinesh and Jian arguing with each other.'

'It makes sense. Jian must have followed Mei.'

'How do you know?' John quizzes her.

Avoiding eye contact with John, Jenny recounts, 'Mei, told me that Jian had got hold of her phone and was fiddling with it.'

'So, what do you think happened?'

'Jian is a jealous person, he must have put a GPS tracker in her iPhone.'

'We can't find the phone.'

Jenny resumes, ' I don't know where the phone is. Mei used to put all the data from her iPhone and MacBook Air on cloud.'

'So we need to find her MacBook Air as well, Guv,' blurts John.

Nikki gently coaxes Jenny for more information, 'What else can you tell us about Mei?'

Jenny's lips quiver as she slumps on the stool, 'Mei's father is a businessman in Hong Kong, her mother is a housewife. You may have found out she was Miss Hong Kong 2017 and Runner Up in Miss World. She wanted to pursue acting and modelling, making loads of money, but...'

More tears well up as she fumbles for a Kleenex in her bag, 'Her father wanted Mei to become a doctor and look after the needy.'

'Capitalism vs. socialism,' titters John.

Jenny ignores his comments, 'Mei used to get a fixed sum each month, which didn't fit with her luxurious life style.'

'I see,' Nikki replies, 'She had to find another source of income.'

'Yes. Although Dinesh came from a rich family, he

couldn't buy her gifts every day.'

John goads her, 'So she needed another way of making some cash?'

Jenny couldn't ignore him anymore, 'Yes and Jian was ready to step in.'

'Last question, Jenny,' Nikki scratches her head thoughtfully.

'OK.'

'Do you think Mei had a bigger appetite for sex?'

Jenny replies with a tight-lipped smile, 'Yes, Mei was a nympho, and she knew it. She schemed to make money.'

'How exactly?' Nikki asked.

'Well', Jenny raises an eyebrow, mischievously dishing the dirt, 'She also had others who could satisfy her desire and buy her worldly goods.'

John can barely disguise his distaste, 'Do you mean to say, she was selling her body?'

'Well, what should I say? She was using her enterprise skill.'

Nikki leans forward, 'Are there other men in Mei's life?'

'I know there were at least two older men. One of

them strong, who could satisfy her appetite and provide money and the other who simply gave her money.'

'Sugar daddy, you mean.' John purses his lips in obvious disapproval.

'Thank you for your time, Jenny, we will come back to you,' says Nikki extending her hand.

12

John opens the door to his Subaru XV to let Nikki in. She smiles, 'Chivalry is not dead then!'

'No, ma'am. I'm an old-fashioned geezer! I open doors for women even though there is equal opportunity and a #me too movement going on.'

'Thank you. Let's go to the Metro University.'

They arrive at the impressive, ultramodern university campus that is divided into two faculties: medicine and engineering. Its construction on a former golf course upset a lot of neighbours who were annoyed by the increased traffic in their quiet neighbourhood.

Two entrepreneurs, David Rowbotham and Sir Timothy Raines, used their expertise to establish the first private university which offers medical and engineering faculties. They ploughed considerable investment into building the state-of-the-art university campus, regrettably, two weeks before it opened, Mr Rowbotham died of a heart attack. Sir Timothy bought his dead partner's shares and took over management of the academies.

'How much do you know about this university?'

'Not much,' fumbles John.

'There is so much demand to study here that students and their families will pay an annual fee of £60 K, far more than the £36 K charged by other universities.'

'Why this sudden urge for private tertiary education?' probes John.

'I call it enterprise and opportunities.'

'I call it greed!' throwing his hands in the air.

'Wow. Looks like you've got a sense of guilt.'

'Perhaps. You may have already googled my mother and know that I come from a rich family.'

'Why do you feel guilty?

'Shouldn't I?'

'Do you live in your parents house?'

'No.'

'Do you ask for money?'

'No.'

'Are you planning to return the money which your parents invested in your education?'

'Fortunately, I had scholarships and my parents didn't fork out any money for fees but they paid for my digs when I was studying.'

'Do you want to pay them back?'

'Maybe one day.'

'You shouldn't be ashamed of who you are, John.'

'We'll talk about it some other time.'

As they enter the Engineering Faculty building, Nikki points at a plaque on the wall which read:

Engineering Faculty

Metro University

Officially opened by

The Hon Anna Williamson MP

Home Secretary UK

'Care to explain this, John?' Nikki is unable to resist teasing.

'Can't help it, Guv, my mum is all over the place like a rash!' John shrugs.

'Don't be so harsh on your mother. She has worked hard to become a successful politician and you should be proud of her.'

'If you say so.'

They ask the receptionist to direct them to the class where Dinesh Malhotra is studying. Looking up from her computer, she advises them that Dinesh had gone on a factory visit with his class and would be back tomorrow.

They return to the car and Nikki sends a message to Dinesh:

Please attend police station in Steely Lane, Birmingham at 10:00 a.m.

Ask for DI Nikki Barnes

This is regarding Mei Wang

Don't ignore

URGENT

'Where to now, Guv?'

'Han Li Supermarket, since our friend, Jian Li, is not answering his phone.'

John pulls onto Bristol Road South in the direction of the Chinese Quarter, a seven-mile trip. He drives past the busy Pershore Road into Hurst Street, famous for the Birmingham Hippodrome, and nabs the last parking space in front of the Han Li Supermarket.

As Nikki enters the shop, the years roll away, the sights and sounds trigger fond childhood memories of the South Korean supermarket she frequented with her parents. The heady smells of the bakery engulf her, overcoming the competing whiff from the fresh fish and meat counters. Her eyes rove greedily over the rows of vegetables and seaweeds, drinking in the aromatic spices, tofu and mushrooms. She could hardly resist the counters stacked with roast pork, poached chicken and stewed octopus.

The Han Li establishment followed the usual Chinese supermarket lay out. In addition to the produce section, there were fresh fish in tanks, crabs crawling over each other in baskets and a plastic barrel of live frogs.

As they enter, John shudders, 'Guv, look at that bloke in the apron covered in blood stains and dirt - he's serving on the meat counter!'

'Don't worry, John, we aren't buying anything here.'

They ask the cashier to page Jian Li.

'No Jian Li here', she counters in a heavy Chinese accent.

'OK. We're police,' John flashes his warrant card, 'Please get your manager.'

The woman makes an announcement on the tannoy in Mandarin.

Nikki bellows in Mandarin, 'I'll arrest you and everyone working here if you try to warn Jian Li again.'

The cashier is flabbergasted to hear Nikki speak fluent Mandarin and so is John.

She leads them to the office behind a stained plastic screen and introduces them to Liu Wei, which means great in Chinese. Nikki muses, this squat person doesn't look capable of doing anything great.

She asks him in Mandarin, 'Where is Jian Li?'

It astounds him to see an Indian looking woman speaking fluent Mandarin, he responds in English, 'He's gone to Manchester for work and you won't be able to get him on his mobile.'

'Thank you, Mr Wei, we want him to come to the police station in Steely Lane at 10:30 a.m.'

'What has he done?' shouts Wei.

'Not for you to know,' retorts John.

Hearing this commotion, a short, plump guy with an oily complexion walks in and bellows, 'What's going on?'

John asks, 'Who are you?'

'I'm Han Li, the owner, and who are you?'

'Police.'

'I know the local police. You're not one of them. Get out,' he roars.

Nikki attempts to reassure him in polite Mandarin, she explains who they are and shows him her warrant card.

Han Li shrugs his shoulders, 'What do you want from my son?'

'Sorry. We can't tell you that. Please send him to the police station tomorrow.'

'OK, I will do that', he gesticulates impatiently at them as if to say get out.

Nikki and John stand outside the supermarket and look around the complex that Han Li has built: a laundry, casino, betting shop, Chinese theatre, a street eatery and a Michelin star restaurant - a massive empire!

As they drive away, they pass the Birmingham Hippodrome, a neo-classical auditorium with a seating capacity of 1,900. Nikki remembers watching several musicals there with her mother.

Her thoughts are interrupted by a call from Dr Freeman, 'Hello, detective. Are you OK to talk?'

'Yes, Dr Freeman. Please go ahead.'

'OK, so, my postgraduate did extraordinary work on

the faeces sample.'

'Yes, I'm listening.'

'He found that the dog was fed on lamb chops and the DNA extraction of the faeces material showed that the hound is an Australian sheep dog.'

'That's great. Please thank your postgraduate for this extraordinary work. It will help us.'

'What was that about?' asks John.

'Oh, it was the turd, sorry, Dr Freeman, talking about the turd which belongs to an Australian sheepdog that ate lamb chops.'

'I'm lost.'

'Don't worry,' Nikki's mind moves up a gear.

13

Nikki puts on her leather jacket and rides off, her phone rings on the blue tooth earpiece.

It was Neha.

'Hi Nikki, is it OK to talk?'

'It is. How are you? How's work?

'Everything with me is fine. It's your brother.'

Neha is the ex wife of her brother, Andrew.

'What about Andrew?'

'He's been beaten up'

'Neha, is my mum with you?'

'No.'

'Don't tell her. I'll be there in 20 minutes.'

Nikki and her younger brother, Andrew, had shared a traumatic upbringing. They both attended Gilbert's Academy in Kings Heath that specialised in children with special needs. They used to be dropped off early each morning to their child minder, Keisha Belinfante. She would run them to and from their school and look after them until their mother picked them up after work in the evening.

The daily routine was always the same. They would pile into Keisha's little hatchback and have a great laugh in the back seat with her son, Delroy, who was the same age as Andrew. Nikki and Andrew were dropped off at school first, then Delroy.

Nikki remembers how Andrew would entertain them in the back of the car with a hilarious impersonation of Keisha and her patois, Jamaican Creole.

He was good at kiss teeth, the Jamaican art of sucking air through the teeth creating a noise which signals disapproval or irritation, often employed by Keisha when one of the children annoyed her. Nikki couldn't master it until she left school.

Andrew suffered from mood swings. The neighbourhood kids were quick to pick up on that and used to call him and Nikki "retards". Andrew would rise to the bait and lash out, but when the local boys came to beat him up, Delroy, who was strong for his age, would always fight them off.

It was a difficult time for the children as their mum, Madhuri Dixit-Barnes, worked long hours as a GP in the busy Small Heath area. She was rarely at home to listen to their problems so, in a way, Keisha was their mother and Delroy like a younger brother.

Keisha met Glenroy Da'Costa, a tall and handsome

Jamaican boxer. The kids were left to their own devices whilst Keisha was tucked up in bed with him.

And why shouldn't Keisha have a good time? She was a young vivacious woman, tall, slim with dark eyes and a wicked sense of humour. If Andrew was naughty, she would tease, 'Cum yah, you coolie boy' a derogatory term used to describe Indians who were farmed out to the West Indies during the British Raj to work on sugarcane plantations.

Glenroy, in contrast, was a morose, quick-tempered hustler, gambler and small-time drug dealer who had no qualms about living off unemployment benefits. He was always there, a glowering presence, when Nikki and Andrew's mother dropped them off at Keisha's house early in the morning. There was an understanding that the kids would not talk about "the boyfriend" to their mother.

After school, Nikki and Andrew returned to Keisha's house till their mother picked them up at 6:30 or 7 p.m. They used to play cricket, kick around a football and, when dinner was ready, devour the heavenly Jamaican dishes cooked by Keisha.

Nikki liked to help Keisha in the kitchen, particularly when Ackee and Saltfish was on the menu. It was a quick meal and her task was to de-bone the fish. For the kids' birthdays, Keisha used to make other Jamaican delicacies like curried chicken, rice and peas, or jerk pork, which they would scoff with relish and the dish washing duties were then handed over to Nikki whilst the boys played outside.

To begin with, Glenroy was friendly and would have a laugh with the kids, but, as time went by, he became moody and aggressive.

Quite out of the blue, about six months after he moved in, Glenroy took the kids to school. To their surprise, Nikki and Andrew were dropped off at a new special school. It didn't seem such a bad move, after all the amiable white-coated staff greeted them each morning with ice cream on arrival. In the afternoon, the special school's driver, Carmen, would drop them off at Keisha's. Nikki would head gratefully for Keisha's warm welcome. There was something impalpable about Carmen's forbidding presence and a peculiar glint in her eye which made Nikki uncomfortable.

It wasn't until much later in life that Nikki began to suspect that there had been something sinister afoot at the school. She surmised that the delicious ice cream concealed sedatives and suddenly it made sense of the mysterious bruise marks that would appear on their forearms.

All these half remembered childhood images and thoughts whirl in Nikki's mind as she makes her way to Neha's flat. Before she knows it, she is riding along the A38 Aston Expressway towards Spaghetti Junction. The locals' nickname for this notoriously complicated road traffic interchange connecting the M6 motorway was apt; traffic was already building up along its tortuous arteries. Her Ducati purrs along, weaving in and out of the jam in Tyburn Road, she whizzes along Eachelhurst Road and soon arrives in Walmley village.

Neha and Andrew shared a two bedroom apartment in Walmley until Andrew came out and proclaimed his love for Ashish Mehra, a thirty something successful lawyer.

The separation was amicable, but Nikki's mother, Madhuri, felt she had failed her son and Neha. If only her work had not been all consuming perhaps she might have picked up on the signals, but she was never at home. Not once had Keisha mentioned that this might be an issue, she was unapproachable on the subject anyway as the Jamaican tradition in which she grew up did not accept the LGBT community.

Andrew had shown no sign of same sex interest whilst growing up, but there were small hints which Nikki could have picked up on; he never had a girl friend until Neha, he didn't ogle at girls or seem interested in girls at all. 'Too late now,' Nikki thinks.

After leaving Neha, Andrew moved into Ashish's stunning home in Little Aston in the leafy suburbs of Sutton Coldfield. It was a luxurious six-bedroom house, which boasted a swimming pool and a Jacuzzi. It wasn't all plain sailing however. Ashish's mother died of a heart attack two years ago. The relatives unjustifiably attributed her death to Ashish coming out as gay.

However, it was not the case as she had already had two heart bypass operations before he became involved with Andrew.

Andrew and Ashish are sitting in Neha's lounge nursing their wounds; bandaged heads and bruises on the forearms.

Nikki gives Andrew a gentle hug, 'What happened to you both?'

Ashish looks up with tears in his eyes and Andrew stutters, 'We were beaten up by a group of men for being gay!'

'Where was this?'

'In front of Ernie's Night club.'

'The one on Mere Green road?'

'Yes, the same,' mumbles Ashish.

'I see you have been looked after by the paramedics. Have you reported it to the police?'

'You're the police. We're not reporting this,' quivers Andrew.

Neha leaned closer to both men, 'This is a hate crime and should be reported to the police.'

Ashish trembles with indignation, 'Who really cares

about these crimes? We'll just be numbers in the Crown Prosecution Service files to be spewed up in their annual statistics.'

Nikki feels a crushing sadness in her chest and urges them again, 'You must report it.'

'No. We won't!' Ashish thumps the coffee table with his fist.

Neha gives Ashish a hug and touches Andrew's right arm gently in an attempt to console them.

Nikki is surprised to find that Neha has matured so much since the initial despair of her marriage breakdown and is now a pillar of strength to her ex.

'Kudos girl,' she murmurs.

She makes a pot of tea for everyone and, after a fraught discussion, they agree that no action would be taken and they disperse.

But Nikki is determined not to leave this alone.

Later that evening, she sits outside Ernie's nightclub, sips from her hip flask and hacks into the club's CCTV camera. The footage shows four men beating up Andrew and Ashish and then driving off in a Mercedes sports car.

She opens the police national computer software on her laptop to check the name of the owner of the Mercedes.

In a matter of minutes, she also finds out that one of the assailants, Mark Spilsbury, is tweeting from a nearby pub about his favourite beer.

She waits outside the pub, silently seething with anger. Her patience is rewarded as Mark and his mates lurch out of the pub and drive off.

Accelerating fast, she easily overtakes their car, skids to a halt and releases a grappler with an extended high strength nylon net. It tangles up the car's front wheels and stops it dead.

The four guys are dazed and stagger out to look at the damage.

Seemingly out of nowhere, a person in a ski mask appears, armed with a collapsible metal baseball bat, and beats the four mercilessly, delivering broken ribs, limbs and shattered patella's.

Before anyone can react, the net is removed and the vigilante disappears into the darkness.

Nikki removes the ski mask, cleans the baseball bat, pushes the bike for almost a mile, then starts the engine and rides off.

No one reports the incident.

14

The welcome aroma of freshly brewed coffee greets Nikki as she enters the room only to find Ayesha, tears coursing down her cheeks, apparently paralysed with fear.

'What's the matter Ayesha?'

'Nothing.'

'You sure?'

Yes. Must be my period pains!' Ayesha tries, unsuccessfully, to brush away Nikki's concern.

'It's more than that. What is it?' probes Nikki.

'He's back!'

'Who? Your ex husband? I thought he went to Dubai after the divorce.'

'What divorce? He texted me Talaq Talaq Talaq and that was my divorce!'

Nikki sighs and pulls up a chair, I know that's an outrageous way to get a divorce, but I thought he'd moved on since then?'

Wiping away her tears, Ayesha can barely voice her fear, 'Yes, I thought so too, but he can still ask to see his son, Hamid, anytime.'

'How did he sound?' Nikki runs her hand nervously through her hair, assuming the worst as she quizzes Ayesha.

'Badrul, my ex, wants to see Hamid and take him to Dubai.'

'Does Hamid want to go with his dad? Do you want him to go?'

'No and no!' screams Ayesha, beside herself with impotent rage.

Just then, John walks in, 'Morning all. What's all this shouting, Ayesha?'

'Nothing, John, I was just in hysterics laughing at Nikki's comments,' she makes a supreme effort to hold back the tears.

'Didn't sound like it!'

'It was a stupid joke, John. Let's get on with our interviews,' soothes Nikki.

As they walk towards the interview room, Nikki sends a message to Ayesha:

"We will sort this out. Don't worry"

The duty officer informs Nikki that a certain Dinesh Mathur has arrived and is in interview room 4.

Nikki introduces herself and John, then immediately begins to size up Dinesh. Tall, slim and fit, straight nose and designer stubble, he had a paler complexion than she had expected, must be of north Indian origin she thinks. Dressed in a grey Canali suit, crisp white shirt, expensive silk tie and shiny Tom Ford shoes, he was the picture of understated elegance. Warm brown eyes steadily returned her gaze.

He sits upright and composed in the chair, arms at his side, the sign of a relaxed man with nothing to hide.

She begins, 'This is not a formal interview, so please tell me a little about yourself.'

John learnt this standard technique at police academy: engage the suspect in light conversation to establish the character of the subject. Whilst asking non-threatening questions, look for tell tale signs: is the subject nervous, scared, prone to bragging, confident? Aim to keep the interrogation more like a relaxed conversation to encourage cooperation and elicit the suspect's motivation.

Dinesh's deep modulated voice conveys the air of an educated, confident person, 'My name's Dinesh Mathur, a first-year student in engineering at the Metro University. I was born and brought up in Nottingham and came here to Birmingham to begin my career as an engineer.'

He pauses.

'Please continue,' Nikki pushes a glass of water towards him.

'What else do you want to know? And what about Mei? Why did you leave me a message about her?'

Nikki plays nonchalantly with her phone, 'Would you mind telling us a little bit about Mei and your relationship with her?'

Dinesh leans back in the chair, takes a deep breath, 'Mei and I have been going out for four months.'

'So, you're in a relationship then?' John suggests.

'If you call going out on a few dates a relationship, then I am in one.'

Nikki realises he is a smart cookie, 'Would you say you have a deep relationship?'

'You mean, do we have a sexual relationship?'

'Yes.'

'We have a sexual relationship, and I'm in love with her,' he mumbles, shifting uncomfortably in his chair.

'How far has your relationship gone?'

'What do you mean gone?' he adjusts his tie

nervously.

'Can you tell me what happened in Devil's Den with Mei two days ago?'

Dinesh sits back, blotting his forehead with a handkerchief, 'I met Mei in Devil's Den, she was drinking alone. We went outside after drinking a glass of champagne.'

'We know that,' John interjects. 'What happened outside?'

'It's embarrassing,' he pauses and looks down at his hands.

'Go ahead. We're all grown up,' smiles Nikki.

'Mei was spontaneous and sexed. We went out, and she gave me oral sex!' He blushes.

'OK. Next?

'We went back inside the club and this Chinese bloke comes over and starts to argue with me.'

'What did he say?'

'He asked me what I was doing with his girlfriend.'

'I told him, the last time I saw her, she was MY girlfriend.'

Nikki nods.

'He got nasty and started a fight. Then the bouncers came over and separated us.'

'So where was Mei during this time?' asks John.

'I don't know. She left the club during the fracas and I haven't seen her since.' Dinesh scratches his nose.

'Did you try to ring her?'

'Yes, a dozen times and each time it went straight to voicemail.'

Nikki watches carefully to gauge his reaction as she breaks the news gently, 'I'm sorry to inform you that Mei is dead. We found her body two days ago.'

Dinesh jumps to his feet, chair crashing backwards to the ground, 'No. It can't be true!' his chest rises and falls with rapid breaths, 'No, not my Mei. But how?' Unstoppable tears of grief well up in his eyes.

John realises the tears are genuine, but still wants to probe, 'Did you kill Mei?'

Dinesh grips the edge of the table and shouts, 'I loved Mei. I wanted to marry her. Why would I kill her?' and slumps into the chair.

'Maybe you found out that you were not the only love in her life and you had a competitor!' challenges John. 'You said earlier the Chinese bloke claimed that Mei was his girlfriend.'

'No, I didn't dispute his claim any further, the confrontation just escalated into a fight. Why would I kill her? I loved her,' he begins to sob.

John sits up and asks, 'So what did you do after you couldn't find Mei in the club?'

'I looked around for ten minutes and then left for my digs.'

'What did you do next?'

'I wrote my assignment and played on my PS4.'

'Can anyone vouch for you?'

'No. I was on my own.'

'Did you have your phone with you all the time?' Nikki asks.

'Yes. It was on as I was hoping Mei would call me when she had cooled down.'

'Did you try to ring her?'

'Yes, a dozen times and each time it went straight to voicemail.'

Nikki touches his arm as if to console him, 'I'm sorry for your loss. That wraps up the interview for now, but please be available for further questioning.'

'Of course. I'll be in Birmingham,' his voice breaks, 'Please find out who killed my Mei and why.'

As Dinesh leaves the room, John turns to Nikki, 'Guv, you were too soft on him.'

'John, my hunch was that he was telling the truth.'

'Come on. He could just have been a good actor.'

'Did you see any signs of sympathetic system activity?'

'You what?'

'Was there any sign of restlessness, sweaty palms and forehead, was he nervous?'

'Umm,' John seems unsure.

'He came dressed smartly.'

'Either he's a consummate liar or he's telling the truth.'

'We'll see.'

'Let's grab a coffee before we see Jian Li.'

Ayesha enters the coffee room and calls over to Nikki, 'I phoned Jonathan Webley.'

'Who?' shouts John from the other end of the room.

'He was the first witness on the scene of the crime.'

'Yes, and?'

'He told me he fed his dog dry food and never gave

it raw meat.'

'Yay, another crime solved,' smirks John.

'It's a good clue John, we should look into it,' Nikki says, sipping her coffee.

15

At midday Jian Li, accompanied by his lawyer, Samuel Morden, breeze into the interrogation room. Nikki gestures for them to take a seat across the table from her and John.

Jian Li plops his squat muscular body down on the chair with an air of superiority, hands stuffed in his pockets, a contemptuous sneer flits across his face. Nikki is struck by his brash, arrogant manner but she is unruffled by his self-confident swagger.

He sports a Samurai bun, the few stray strands of hair, which hang over his forehead, do nothing to moderate his hard angular facial features. Plastic surgery had straightened his nose and achieved a slightly softer facial contour.

Two infamous Chinese triad tattoos adorn his neck and wrist; a dragon and phoenix represent the balance of yang and ying. The dragon depicts the yang or dark side of power and control, whilst the phoenix symbolises regeneration and power.

Jian Li's ostentatious wardrobe is designed to impress; the Bottega Veneta leather aviator jacket must have cost him a cool £5000, Balmain jeans and a Hublot Black Caviar Big Bang wrist oozed millionaire exclusivity - a gift from an indulgent father, perhaps.

Nikki has to tear herself away from analysing the display of wealth on this young man's body. She kicks off the interview with a brief introduction.

Jian Li skips the niceties and in his adenoidal voice brazenly demands, 'Why have you called me here? What right did you have to come to my business yesterday?'

Noting that Jian's hands tighten into fists as he speaks, John keeps his tone even but firm, 'Mr Li, we want to know about your whereabouts two nights ago and how well you know Mei Wang.'

Looking away, Jian Li undid his ponytail, retied it and blurted, 'Mei Wang is my girlfriend. I was at home playing video games two nights ago.'

'Tell us more about your relationship with Mei.'

'We've been going out to night clubs and the cinema.'

'Do you fight?'

'Like in any relationship we fight but then we make up, ' he chuckles.

'How do you make up Mr Li?'

'This is a personal question and you can't ask that,' interjects the solicitor.

'It's not a tricky question, Mr Morden.'

'OK,' toying with a lock of his hair, Li continues, 'We're lovers. We fight and make up with steamy sex sessions.'

Nikki intervenes, 'Did you have sex two days ago?'

Li chortles, 'We had sex late morning in her flat.'

'Then?'

'I left for the casino.'

'When did you see her again?'

'I found out she was at Devil's Den and decided to surprise her that evening.'

'Did you surprise her?'

'Yes and so was I!' he lets out a harsh gasp of indignation.

'How?'

'Mei was with an Indian bloke, drinking champagne,' he gives a mirthless laugh.

'Did you feel angry?' John asks.

'Wouldn't you, mate, if your bird was with someone else?' he snarls, drawing a finger across his throat.

John finds the threatening gesture offensive and also the implication that his girlfriend might be with someone else. He doesn't respond but finds himself wondering what Tina was doing. He had not heard from her all day.

Nikki resumes, 'So, Mr Li, what happened when you saw Mei with this man?'

'I told her that I don't like two-timing women,' he rubs his chin ruefully.

'What did she say?'

'Nothing. She began to tremble and the Indian bloke shouted at me.'

'What did he say exactly?'

'That she was his girlfriend and I should back off.'

'How did you take it?'

Li stiffened and shouted, 'I was angry. I really lost it. He threw a punch at me and I thumped him. Then the bouncers stopped the fight.'

'What happened then?'

'I left the club.'

'Did you see Mei?'

'No. I was upset that my girlfriend was cheating on me.'

'Where did you go?'

'Home.'

'And?'

'I played on my PS4 with friends in Hong Kong.'

John had composed himself by this time, 'So you didn't see Mei after the fight?'

'No!' screams Li. 'I didn't see her.'

'Did you kill Mei Wang, Mr Li?'

'You can't ask this question detective,' Morden gives John a steely glance, 'What proof have you got?'

Nikki butts in, 'Sorry about this Mr Morden and Mr Li. Just two questions. Did you use a condom for sex with Mei?'

'No, why should I? She was on the pill.'

'Second question. Have you got an alibi for that evening?'

'Yes, I was playing with three other guys who are in Hong Kong.'

The enormity of the situation suddenly hits Li, his face crumples as the reality of Mei's death sinks in.

Nikki expresses her sympathy, 'I'm sorry for your loss. You're free to go after giving a swab for DNA analysis.'

Li's bullish demeanour cracks, he covers his face with his hands and finally the tears come.

16

Nikki, John and Ayesha meet up with the DCI after lunch for a quick rundown of progress so far.

Ayesha reads from her laptop, 'Dinesh was telling the truth. I triangulated his phone signals. They show that after he left Devil's Den he didn't move from his digs all evening and the entire night.'

'What about Jian Li?'

'Same here, sir. He left the club and his phone signals indicate that he was also at his home address all evening. There's something else!'

'Yes, what?'

'Sir, he was using the share play on his Play Station 4 machine with three other friends from Hong Kong.'

DCI Hill had earned the unkind label of technotard in the station, he had failed to move with the times and was painfully technically challenged, a true computer dummy, 'How do you know this?'

'Sir, we logged into Mr Li's server which was sending and receiving information from other players with different IP addresses. His router gave us the details. He's been telling the truth.'

'So, neither Dinesh nor Jian were near the Lickey Hills,' concludes Hill.

'That's correct, sir.'

'OK, DI Barnes and DC Williamson find out about the DNA results and follow any other leads.'

'Yes, sir.' Nikki gestures a thumbs up.

17

Nikki opens her laptop and emails Badrul Hussain, enticing him to open a link with interesting material.

Once his computer becomes active, and he opens the link, it drops a payload.

He is completely unaware of what is coming next.

18

Nikki rides into the city centre and parks her bike in the Bull Ring Shopping Centre. She remembers her mother telling her about the origin of the name, Bull Ring. In the 1730s, this area was known as Corn Cheaping. The green within Corn Cheaping was used for bullbaiting and the 'ring' was a hoop of iron to which they tied bulls for baiting before slaughter. The first Bull Ring shopping centre, built in 1964, was demolished and replaced by the present brand new swanky mall in 2003.

Nikki makes her way to the toilets on the first floor where she assumes a new persona. She changes into a tatty top, worn out jeans and grimy flat pumps. Checking her appearance in the long mirror for the desired effect, she grins: down at heel and down on her luck. Perfect.

From the escalator, Nikki admires the myriad of shops selling clothes and jewellery. A life size hoarding of an Indian cricketer catches her eye, advertising an expensive flashy watch. She pushes her way through the exit and into the crowded piazza. Some tourists are busy taking selfies in front of the iconic 2.2 metre high bronze sculpture of the eponymous bull. The place is bustling with people of Asian, African and Eastern European origin, many of them laden with large paper bags bearing the name of the famous low cost, no frills high shop. Others are more interested in pedalling religion than goods. A cacophony of different prophets vie for attention, noisily promoting their beliefs as the one true faith and handing out literature. The passers by dodge them as well as the inevitable market researchers, but pause to take in the free street show of some hip-hop enthusiasts.

As she enters the high street, she observes a young man in his 20s, squatting, still as a statute, staring vacantly at the wall. Without doubt he is experiencing the destructive side effects of a new form of cannabis, spice, or black mamba, currently plaguing the streets of the UK. A recent police briefing informed staff about new legislation designed to facilitate charging users. The speaker gave a graphic account of how spice mimics the effects of cannabis, but is far more potent causing distressing side effects, leaving users vulnerable while under the influence of the drug.

A few metres further along, another homeless man crouches in the side entrance of a famous bookshop with his Staffordshire bull terrier, a flat cap on the ground containing some coins.

Nikki gently strokes the dog, 'Hey, how are you?'

Drawing in a long breath, he pulls the dog's chain as if to protect it and grunts suspiciously, 'Yeah, what do you want?'

Tugging her earlobe, Nikki persists, 'Where are you from?'

'What's it to you? You ain't from the council!' He rubs his eyes, looking around anxiously.

Nikki notices his fidgety erratic manner and realises that he is due his fix any moment, 'Want to try some of my dope?'

'You're kidding me?'

'Why not?' she sits next to him, jiggling her foot.

'OK,' he relaxes, 'You ain't a pig, are you?'

Nikki laughs dismissively, 'Do I look like one?' she leans closer and hands over a small packet.

'Can't trust no one!' he mutters rolling the weed Nikki gave him.

He strokes his dog and shoots her a suspicious look, 'I know there's no such thing as a free lunch. What do you want?'

Picking at her nails, she asks, 'Do you know a bloke with an Australian sheep dog?'

Inhaling the weed, he demands, 'Why do you want to know about him?'

'Do you know him?' she leans closer to him.

The dog growls a warning to keep her distance.

'OK, cool it, I'm not doing anything to your master!' she says, looking at the dog.

'He's protective of me. Anyway, why are you asking about this guy?'

'Well,' putting her hands on her hips, 'I've seen him twice and, you know,' she gives him a knowing look and chuckles.

'You know what?'

'OK. Do I have to spell it out?'

'Yes!' bellows the man.

'I went to bed with him twice, but I don't know his name or where he lives.'

'The naughty Romeo!'

'If you say so,' she shrugs.

'His name is Sam. He has an Australian sheepdog.'

'What else can you tell me about him?'

'Didn't he tell you?'

'No, we didn't have time for pillow talk!' she titters.

'He's a squaddie. Fought in Afghanistan.'

'Do you know the name of his regiment?'

Running his hand over the dog and then scratching his armpit, he says, 'I think he was in undercover ops.'

'Did he tell you anything specific?'

'No!' he loses patience with the conversation.

'Sorry. I didn't mean to annoy you.'

Smirking, he giggles, bobbing his head, 'You talk like a posh bird!'

'I didn't want to piss you off. Sorry,' nevertheless she continues to probe, 'Does he have any family?'

'Are you sure, you're not a cop?'

I'm a jealous woman. I don't like competition.'

'I think he's separated. That's all I know.'

'Where can I find him?'

'Either in the shelter in Ward End or under the bridge in Hockley.'

'Thanks mate,' Nikki presses a fiver into his hand.

If I see Sam, shall I tell him you were looking for him?'

'Don't worry. I'll find him.'

The dishevelled man gratefully pockets the note and strokes the dog curled up by his side. All this time the dog had kept a silent watch, staring at them both as if he understood everything that passed between them.

Wearing the same outfit, Nikki rides to the shelter in the Hodge Hill area of Ward End, east of the city.

The receptionist, an Afro-Caribbean in her 50s, eyes Nikki with suspicion, rests her ample bosom on the counter and demands, 'what do you want with Sam? Who are you?'

'I'm Sam's friend,' Nikki reassures her.

'I haven't seen Sam with any girlfriends. You're telling lies!' she looks hard at Nikki.

'No. I'm telling the truth. I saw him a few weeks ago, at my place near Digbeth.'

'Sam hasn't been seen at the shelter for the last few days.'

'What about his dog?'

'Oh, Ruby?' enquires the receptionist.

'Yes, Ruby.'

'Sweet sheepdog. She's in the kennels for the homeless in Stechford.'

Nikki makes her way to the kennels in Stechford and tells a convincing story about doing research on dogs kept by homeless people. She finds Ruby sitting forlornly in the corner of a pen.

Nikki had done some preliminary research about Australian sheepdogs. It seems they had a lot in common with English Shepherds and Border Collies: eager to please and valued for their skills and obedience.

Ruby looks well nourished, considering her owner is a homeless person. She weighed around 25 kilos and had liver merle with a copper tan on her face, chest and legs. Her long, wavy coat seemed to be in reasonably good condition.

For an intelligent dog which loves to play and learn, Ruby looks depressed, sitting miserably in a corner, an obvious sign that she was missing her master!

Nikki enquires at the reception, 'Does this dog eat dry food or meat?'

The volunteer attendant looks bored, she shrugs, 'I don't know what she eats. I can check.'

'Please do!'

She opens the database and confirms, 'Ruby eats meat, but in this kennel, we only feed the dogs dry food.'

'Do you have the owner's details?'

The receptionist's suspicions are aroused, 'You don't look like a cop. who are you?' she scowls.

'Of course I'm not a cop,' Nikki snaps,

'I'm the owner's girlfriend. I've lost Sam's phone number.'

'Sorry, but because of GDPR, I can't give out personal details,'

'What's that?'

The receptionist patiently intones, 'GDPR stands for General Data Protection Regulation and it means we cannot divulge any personal details.'

Nikki feigns a sudden loss of energy and leans on the counter muttering, 'Hypo, I need sugar and water.'

The girl knows very well the implications of a hypo; she certainly doesn't want any incidents on her watch so she scoots off to fetch water and a lump of sugar.

While the volunteer is distracted, Nikki looks at the database and commits Sam's telephone number to memory.

After drinking the sugary water, she thanks the volunteer, waves goodbye to Ruby and leaves.

Nikki opens her palmtop, enters Sam's number and triangulates. She knows exactly where he is!

19

It is 05:00 a.m. and something wakes Badrul Hussain up.

'Open the door, otherwise we'll knock it down,' someone bellows from outside.

'Who is it?' Badrul shouts back.

'Police. Open the door.'

Badrul pulls on his pyjamas and opens the door.

Four plain-clothes police officers enter the house and one of them gets hold of the laptop.

The second one shouts, 'Kneel! Arms behind your back!'

'Why? I've done nothing wrong,' pleads Badrul.

'We are arresting you on two charges,' cautions a tall black officer.

'What are they?' stutters Badrul.

'Child pornography and links to extremists.'

'You must be kidding. I'm a decent law-abiding citizen,' pleads Badrul.

'Where's your passport?' yells another officer.

An officer from the kitchen shouts, 'Look, I found three passports here.'

'Wow. Three! How come you own three passports, Mr. Hussain?' shouts the black officer, grabbing hold of Badrul.

'I can't say. I need to speak to my lawyer.'

'OK. Now you want to speak to your lawyer!' The officer gives a bitter laugh.

'What are you charging me with?' a trembling Badrul begs again.

'I have charged you under Section 160, sub subsection 1, for owning indecent photographs or pseudo-photographs of a child or children and...' the officer waits for a reaction from Badrul.

Shoulders slumped, head bowed, Badrul shouts, 'No. It's not true; I'm being stitched up. Who has done this?'

'I need to caution you on a grievous matter of national significance!' the officer continues.

'What?' a crying Badrul asks.

'It links you with terrorist organisations in Syria and Yemen.'

'It can't be. I'm a businessman.'

'We are taking you in for questioning and holding your passports.'

He is whisked away in an unmarked car.

20

Nikki triangulates Sam's phone and locates him under the bridge in Hockley, a seven-mile trip, which in rush hour could take around twenty to twenty-five minutes. She tops up her makeup to maintain her appearance as a homeless waif and rides past Heartlands Parkway and enters Saltley at the roundabout. From there she weaves through the busy rush hour traffic onto Boulton Middleway and reaches Hockley.

In the early evening light Nikki makes out the top of the concrete steps which lead down the side of the bridge towards the canal. She meets two homeless men in their 30s. They walk down the steps alongside Nikki, talking about how their day went. When one of them notices her, he takes out a carton of cigarettes from the front pocket of his torn jacket and offers one to Nikki. She doesn't want to offend him by refusing and as she smokes, joins in their conversation.

She wonders what her friend Ayesha, or even her mother, would think if they saw her in the company of these people. In reality, these men are not hardened criminals but people whose circumstances locked them into a stagnant struggle for life.

Nikki strikes up a conversation, 'Hi, I'm Tessa. Thanks for the ciggie.' She always used Tessa as a back up name, remembering the famous athlete who came from Birmingham.

'Hi, I'm Nate,' replies the guy who offered the cigarette.

'And I'm Tony,' his friend says.

'Lived here long?'

Nate is hunched and looks shorter than his companion, 'I've been here five years and Tony joined us two years ago.'

Tony takes long-legged strides as if in a hurry to do something or go somewhere.

Nikki probes, 'So how did you end up living here?'

Both laugh, 'It's our Crystal who brought us here!'

'You mean crystal meth?'

Tony nods.

'How's life then?'

His cigarette dangles from the corner of his mouth as Nate reflects for a moment, 'We've never been hungry as we scrape together enough from doing odd jobs around the area, like helping the gardeners, painters and decorators.'

'Do you get any handouts?'

Tony grits his teeth and snarls, 'We don't like handouts, we'd rather work and keep our dignity.'

'Have you got a family?' inquires Nikki.

'What's it to you? You don't look like a homeless person. Are you a journalist?' objects Tony, who seems to have a short fuse.

'Do I look like a journalist?' quips Nikki.

In the dim light emanating from the street lamp on the bridge, Nate could make out her svelte body and Nikki's beautiful face which he thought could do with a wash.

Tony twitters, 'Must dash, Tessa, have a date with my Crystal!'

'See you soon guys,' teases Nikki.

She pushes past the bushes growing along the worn dirt trail, jumps over a stagnant pool of rainwater avoiding human faeces and collides with an abandoned supermarket trolley.

A bloke shouts out from the dark, 'Don't touch my trolley or I'll kill you!'

She prods the owner of the voice to ask if Sam is about, to which she gets a garbled response.

Something about the eerie surreal surroundings trigger a vivid recall of her days on active duty in Helmand province. Perhaps it's the pungent smell of weed which assaults her senses as she stumbles over the piles of rubbish, spray cans and vandalised road signs that line the footpath.

A gaunt figure smoking a joint offers, 'What do you want, darlin'? Looking for love? I'll give you some.'

'No thanks. I'm looking for Sam.'

'I'm no good for you then. The squaddie will be here shortly,' he rasps.

'Where's his corner then?' Nikki flirts.

The man doffs his Peaky Blinder cap in mock deference, 'this is the king size bed area for squaddie Sam. You sure you don't want a quickie with me?'

'Maybe some other time,' Nikki lies. She bides her time, drawing on her cigarette.

Her patience is rewarded as a figure resembling Sam appears out of the shadows and shuffles towards his allotted place.

Nikki turns and offers, 'Want some dope?'

'No, thanks. Got my own.' Sam answers guardedly.

'Can I have whatever you're having?'

'Are you sure?'

'Yeah. I am,' she edges closer to him.

'Haven't seen you before. Where did you spring

from?'

'Tessa, from Telford,' she tilts her head towards him.

'What brings you here, then?'

'Same as you.'

'Come on, you can tell me.'

'My husband chucked me out after he caught me smoking dope,' her head droops as she shrugs her shoulders in resignation at her lot.

'Sorry to hear that,' remarks Sam, candidly surveying her slim attractive body.

'What about you?' Nikki licks her lips nervously and settles down next to him.

'Ex soldier, divorced, not much else to say,' Sam responds, sinking heavily onto the damp grass, leaving his mobile phone by his side.

Nikki begs Sam, 'Come on then, you gonna share your dope?'

Sam takes out a sachet, makes three lines of cocaine and gestures to her to snort.

As Nikki leans towards Sam, she's struck by his body odour, the same distinctive smell that she detected near Mei Wang's body.

Whilst appearing to inhale, Nikki ensures that her phone is next to Sam's enabling it to be cloned and introduce a tracker.

A few minutes later, Nikki abruptly excuses herself leaving Sam to sink into a hazy stupor.

Back on the bridge above the canal, Nikki sits astride her bike, checking that Sam's phone is cloned and the tracker is working.

As she is about to start the engine, her phone rings.

'DI Barnes? Superintendent Bob Newton here.'

'Hello, sir. What can I do for you?'

'I have bad news. DCI Hill had a heart attack and they've moved him to the University Hospital for emergency bypass surgery.'

'I'm sorry to hear about DCI Hill, sir.'

'Yes. Now, I'm asking you to take charge of the murder case. You're the acting DCI till I find someone else.'

As Nikki is about to say something, the phone goes dead.

21

Nikki knocks on Ayesha's door.

Startled, Ayesha asks, 'Who is it?'

'Pizza delivery.'

Ayesha recognises the voice, 'We haven't ordered any pizza.'

'Come on. Stop messing about, open the door,' chides Nikki.

Ayesha opens the door, spreads her arms wide in greeting and berates Nikki, 'What time do you call this?'

'You look stunning in those PJs, Ayesha. If I were a man, I swear I wouldn't know what to do,' she winks and touches her arm.

'It's always nice to see you. Anything in particular that brings you here this evening?'

'Yes. I found our first lead and cloned his phone,' handing her phone to Ayesha.

'OK. So you want me to decipher it. Can't it wait till tomorrow morning?' protests Ayesha.

'It could. But Chief Inspector Hill is in the hospital and they made me DCI.'

'OK boss.'

'Yes, so please, my super efficient buddy, now would be a good time,' she wheedles, jumping on Ayesha's bed.

'Make yourself comfortable, madam, why don't you? So, was it you that ratted on Badrul?'

'Moi?' Nikki rolls her eyes.

'Yes, you! Did you plant something on him?'

'Maybe,' Nikki feigns wide-eyed innocence.

'He is the father of my child!'

'I know how he has mistreated you in the past and it was starting all over again,' Nikki crinkles her nose as she explains herself.

'You reek of weed and your pupils look dilated. What have you been up to?'

'I was partying with two guys in Hockley and then snorted with our soldier friend, Sam,' chuckles Nikki, ever so slightly out of it.

'Coming back to Badrul,' interrupts Ayesha.

'Yes, Badrul, father of your son, your first cousin whom your parents forced you to marry,' yells Nikki defensively.

'So,' sulks Ayesha.

'So, he blackmails you for money, rapes you and

when your beautiful son, Hamid, is born with a deformity, he abandons you. What kind of man is he?'

'Hamid has done well,' Ayesha's eyes flood with tears.

'Yes, Ayesha, he's done well, and it's all because of you and you only,' observes Nikki, giving her a hug.

A sobbing Ayesha continues, 'You always warned me about first cousin marriages and the possible impact on children like mood disorders, mental and physical disabilities, even deaths, but I was helpless.'

Nikki tries to comfort her, 'I don't want to say, "I told you so". It's done, Hamid, is a bright kid and his inability to walk has not stopped him from being top of the class and playing sport with his friends.'

'I know that,' she sniffs and tries to compose herself. 'OK. What about this soldier then?'

'He seems to be a nice guy, but in the wrong place because of circumstances.'

'Care to elaborate?'

'Will do so in the morning. Say "Hi" to Hamid, need to catch up with him sometime.'

'You're like an Englishman using such a cliché - must catch up, need to catch up.'

'Well, I am half English,' Nikki laughs with a big
goofy grin.

22

'I am half- English,' the phrase stirred up painful memories.

She recollects travelling from London to Birmingham, at the age of seven, with her younger brother, Andrew. Her mother, Dr Madhuri Dixit Barnes, was driving her Mercedes C class, trying to keep the children entertained with various songs and "I spy with my little eye". Andrew asked his mother why they were moving to Birmingham and why daddy did not come with them. How could Madhuri explain to a five-year-old child that they had been evicted from their own home by her abusive, cheating husband?

Andrew grew increasingly disruptive, swore all the time and would alternate between running back and forth repetitively or rocking movements, which seemed to soothe him somehow. Her mother seemed at a loss as to how to handle his behaviour, sometimes she would cajole him or even spank him but this just made him worse. It was a relief when they met their nanny, Keisha, she had an instinctive way of calming Andrew and defusing tension.

From a young age, Nikki realised there was something wrong with Andrew and to a certain extent with herself, she suffered from frequent seizures and depression. Streams of suicidal and intrusive thoughts plagued her, repetitive behaviours, over which she had little control, used to upset her. On top of this, she developed panic attacks and an uncontrollable urge to run away from people. Her paediatrician at the Children's Hospital later diagnosed her with obsessive compulsive and general anxiety disorder- at last the beginning of a long road to understanding her psyche and an attempt to achieve a satisfying life balance.

Nikki recollects her mother's story: Dr Madhuri Dixit, a budding gynaecologist, arrived from Mumbai, caught the eye of Neville Barnes, a junior doctor specialising in plastic surgery. After a whirlwind romance, they got married in a church in Bath followed by an Indian wedding in Mumbai.

Madhuri opted for general practice training when she found herself pregnant with Nikki. A few years later, she had Andrew. As a little girl, Nikki noticed that her dad never returned home in the evenings. Her mother always had an excuse for his absence. She witnessed disturbing violent arguments between her parents and later watched her mother cover up her black eye with make up.

She remembered her dad, a tall, blond Englishman with ice blue eyes, apparently an ideal catch for any woman. He became a plastic surgeon with a successful practice in Harley Street, London. She had fond memories of him, he particularly doted on her, but sadly as she and Andrew grew older and began to exhibit behavioural problems, Neville distanced himself from them.

When they first arrived in Birmingham, they stayed in a bed and breakfast place for a few months before moving to Sparkbrook, a run down inner city area, where Madhuri could afford to rent a three-bedroom house. It was a convenient location for her as she found a job as a GP in the nearby Small Heath area. It wasn't easy as a single parent holding down a demanding job. To make matters worse, a few months after she began working at the surgery, the senior partner was arrested for embezzling money from the Health Service and she found herself running the practice single handed.

As work became more and more demanding, she found a great ally in Keisha Belinfante, the beautiful Jamaican woman she employed as a nanny for her children.

A ping on Nikki's phone disturbs her train of thought.

Sam the soldier was on the move.

23

John waits for Tina to arrive at Tudors, a Michelin starred restaurant in Edgbaston. He gets a message:

Darling, on my way

Tina xxx

He orders pale ale and opens the mail from his dad marked confidential.

Subject: Nikhila (Nikki) Barnes

Ex Major in the marines and doctor. Saw active duty in Helmand. Operated on nine soldiers with grave injuries - saved all. An active professional soldier. Killed at least fifteen Taliban soldiers.

Childhood and adolescence details sketchy.

One school record entry shows she was bullied in school because of her autism - no further records of other incidents. Parents separated. Father, a successful plastic surgeon, now on his third wife, a Lithuanian beauty queen.

Mother, a general practitioner in an inner city area of Birmingham.

Brother, a banker living with his boyfriend. Nikhila, single, not in a relationship.

John is digesting the information about his boss when Tina arrives, casually plants a kiss on his forehead, plonks herself on the chair and immediately begins checking her messages.

John's mouth sets in a grim tense line, 'Darling, are you going to look at the menu?'

Tina drops her head in her hands and whines, 'You don't want me to succeed, do you?'

'I do!'

'Just leave me alone for a few minutes and order me a Caesar salad,' she purses her lips and scowls as she types.

John snorts with indignation and waves at the waiter to take their order.

Minutes pass by before Tina looks up and seems to remember to ask, 'How was your day?'

John answers with a stony, 'OK.'

'John, we are grown-up people. We need to work hard to succeed, not everyone has a Home Secretary as a mother and retired police commissioner as a father!' taunts Tina sarcastically.

The hurt is written all over his face as his frustration at her indifference and barbed remarks finally boils over.

John protests, 'What's the matter with you, Tina? You hardly acknowledge me; don't you want to be with me? Why don't we ever talk about fixing a date for our marriage?'

Tina's stress is obvious. She looks wide-eyed at John, surprised that he picked her up on her distracted behaviour. Her eyelids twitch a little as she suggests defensively, 'This is not the time to talk about marriage, John. Something incredibly important is happening in my professional life and I can't think of anything else!'

'So work is more important than us?' a surge of pain wells up inside John, his knuckles whiten as he tightens his grip on the arms of his chair.

As she is about to blurt out an answer, the phone rings, her priority is clear, 'I have to take this.'

A few minutes later, she stomps back to the table, cheeks flushed and nostrils flared.

'Is everything all right?' John tries to defuse the tension.

'Let's eat. I don't want to talk about it,' hot tears well up in her eyes. They eat in painful silence.

After they leave the restaurant John is non-plussed by her ambiguous behaviour.

Too many freaky things were happening with Tina for him to ignore.

24

It is 7:30 a.m. and the incident room is full.

'Good afternoon, Ayesha,' Nikki's eyes roll skywards as her colleague walks through the door.

'Sorry, Guv, I was gathering info!' mutters Ayesha.

'What is this Guv business? Where is DCI Hill?' John looks across at Nikki who is sitting at the top of the table.

'Sorry, folks. I have news. DCI Hill had cardiac bypass surgery yesterday and they've asked me to deputise as acting DCI,' announces Nikki.

'Sorry to hear about the DCI,' comments Nina Kowalski, the criminal psychologist.

'Please convey our best wishes to his family,' Harbans Kaur, the data analyst, mumbles.

'Let us start with you, Mr O'Hara.'

Michael O'Hara, an experienced sergeant, clears his throat and begins, 'Door to door enquiries suggest no one saw the victim or perpetrator. We recorded no untoward activity.'

Nikki looks at Daniel Aboah, a civilian of Ghanaian descent, 'What did you find out on CCTV?'

Daniel delivers his report in a thick Ghanaian accent, 'We had trabal making any sense with the CCTV of nighttime. Air are daytime clips from which we are still trying to identify people.'

Nikki is familiar with the idiosyncrasies of his spoken English, trabal was trouble and air was here.'

'Thanks, Daniel. What about you, Ayesha?' Nikki looks at her expectantly.

'Guv, I decoded the phone you gave me.'

'What phone?' John challenges.

'Long story, John. Proceed Ayesha,' Nikki's eyes flash as she tinkers with her pen.

'The phone belongs to Samuel Masterson, a 35 year old ex marine, who fought in Afghanistan. Samuel's wife threw him out of their home in Telford. He was in arrears with payments to the Child Support Agency to the tune of £1,200 and in addition he owed £3,000 plus interest to a money lender.'

'Lot of money to pay,' mumbles John.

'Fortunately for him, someone paid it off two days ago!'

'We'll return to that later, Ayesha. Any more entries in the phone?'

'I logged into his web history which was revealing,' smirks Ayesha.

'Samuel visited the Dark Net and took a job! How many of you know how the Dark Net works?'

Only Nikki raises her hand.

'OK. I'll put us all in the picture.'

She coughs and sips some water, 'the dark net or dark web is an umbrella term used to describe the area of the Internet which is not open to public view. As some of you are aware, it facilitates computer crime and the sale of restricted goods like drugs. It also protects dissidents and whistleblowers.'

'Are we good so far?' she looks up and continues. 'All these networks require the installation of specific software such as Tor or Onion Router. Anyone can access via a customised browser. I discovered that Samuel used a site called AOD, Assassination on Demand.'

'Charming name!' quips Nina.

Ayesha resumes, 'this site uses an onion router, a technique for anonymous communication over a network. In this network, they encapsulate messages in layers of encryption, similar to the layers of an onion. It transmits the encrypted data through a series of network nodes, concealing the origin, destination and content of the activity.'

'Are you on the Dark Net, Ayesha?' quizzes Harbans Kaur with a toothy grin.

'I go on it for official business, not for personal use!' smiles Ayesha.

'Please continue, Ayesha,' says Nikki, pursing her lips.

'Sure, Guv. I hacked into Samuel's password and entered the AOD site and this is what I found.' She links her laptop to the overhead projector and it displays screenshots of Samuel's web history.

AOD

Add a name to the list	Mei Wang
Add money to pot in person's name	2 Bitcoin
Predict when that person will die	
Correct prediction gets the pot	
Make your predictions come true (optional)	

'What is Bitcoin?' asks Nina.

'Bitcoin is electronic cash sent from one user to another on the peer-to-peer network with no intermediaries. At present two Bitcoin are worth £5,300. This transaction allowed Samuel to pay off his debts.'

'I'm perplexed by this process, Ayesha!' complains Nina.

'It's tricky. First, the would-be assassin sends his prediction in an encrypted message locked by a digital code. He then makes the kill and sends the code to the organisation. They use the code to unlock his prediction,' Ayesha pauses.

'How is the money delivered?' asks John.

'Well, once the organisation verifies the assassination by watching the news, they donate the prize money in the form of Bitcoin and it is put online as an encrypted file.'

'So he hasn't got the money, yet?' John looks puzzled.

'Only a key can unlock that file, generated by whoever makes the prediction,' Ayesha explains.

'Bitcoin is not real. How did Samuel convert it to pounds then?' Daniel Aboah challenges.

'There are several Bitcoin ATMs dotted around

Birmingham. He cashed his money in Hockley, an area near to his present location.'

'Is it kept as a secret from everyone?' asks Harbans Kaur.

'Yes. The organisation could verify the prediction and award the prize to the person who made it, with no one knowing anything about it.'

'Except you,' Nikki smiles.

Ayesha's eyes sparkle.

'Let's grab this person, Samuel,' says John clutching his phone.

'Sure, John. We'll pick him up later,' Nikki reassures him.

She looks at the others and concludes, 'We'll meet in an hour to discuss the CCTV footage which we got from Mei Wang's house.'

25

The incident room is buzzing with activity.

Nikki bangs on the table to gain everyone's attention and gestures to Ayesha to start.

The laptop goes live and shows video clips of Mei in compromising positions, having sex with Jian Li, dating back to two days before the murder, and then with Dinesh.

'Are you holding back on something, Ayesha?' enquires Nikki.

'Well. I was trying to build up the climax!'

'Ayesha! It is early morning and you are talking smut,' quips Harbans Kaur, a devout Sikh lady.

'I wasn't, Harbans. Watch this clip.' It shows Han Li, the father of Jian Li and owner of the Chinese Empire in Birmingham, having sex with Mei.

Mei is arguing with Han who is speaking in Mandarin.

John looks up at Nikki, 'Boss, what are they saying?'

Daniel is impressed, 'Don't tell me you can speak Mandarin?'

'Mei wants money and Han is saying that he has

already paid her. She insists that she wants more and now you can see he's getting angry. Now he's saying if you don't stop pestering me, I will kill you,' Nikki completes her running commentary.

Ayesha fast-forwards it and they see Han Li walking towards the bathroom to dispose of his used condom.

Another video starts; this one was recorded twelve hours before the murder. Mei has strapped a man to the bed and she is playing dominatrix. She is flogging this man who is wearing a ski mask and groaning with pleasure.

At the end of the act, Mei shouts at him, 'Who is the boss?'

'You,' moans the man after another lash.

'I need another five thousand pounds,' she hisses.

'Yes, madam. You will have it. Please release me now.'

Ayesha fast-forwards the clip. After Mei releases the man, she gives him a stern look and shouts, 'You will give me that money. OK, baby?'

The man insists, 'I don't have it babe.'

'I don't care. I need the money. If you don't give it to me, you know what will happen!' she delivers her threat with an arrogant swagger.

The man puts on his clothes, still wearing the ski mask. As he leaves, the hidden camera captures a clear image.

It reveals his piercing blue eyes in the slits of the balaclava.

Nikki's tone is decisive, 'John, let's pick up Samuel now and later on we will talk to Han Li.

26

They triangulate Sam's phone to the kennels where his Australian sheepdog, Ruby, is housed.

Nikki arrives at the kennels and shows John that the signals are coming from the courtyard. They see Sam holding Ruby lovingly, close to his chest as if to console her.

Nikki allows Sam to cherish the moment with his dog and as he releases his hold, the dog whirls around licking, jumping and trying to make a fuss of her master. Sam lets this continue but, as Nikki approaches, the dog senses a threat and barks as John draws near.

The dog responds to Nikki's soothing voice wags her tail and settles down next to Sam.

Sam looks up, 'Hello stranger. You've scrubbed up well. Who's this bloke? Is he your boyfriend? How did you find me?'

'Hi, Sam, this is my colleague DC Williamson and I'm acting DCI Nikki Barnes.'

'Oh, the fuzz. What can I do for you?'

'Please come to the station. We have some questions for you.'

Sam hesitates, 'Can I come in a few minutes?' He

caresses Ruby.

'Sure, we'll wait for you,' says Nikki.

'You're allowing time for a suspect?' John gives an incredulous smile.

'Ruby is his soul mate. I want him to spend time with her. He may never see the dog again if proven guilty.'

Sam bids goodbye to Ruby who is now whining, trembling and licking Sam with her tail tucked between her legs.

The dog is led away by the warden and Sam's hand trembles as he reaches for the doorknob.

Sam nurses a cup of coffee in the interview room while Nikki adjusts the recording device. Nina Kowalski and Ayesha stand behind the one-way screen listening to the interview.

'Sam, we want to ask you some questions,' John begins.

'Am I under arrest? Do I need a lawyer?' Sam asks.

'No, you are not under arrest. Just a few questions,' Nikki rubs her chin.

'How can I trust you, DCI Barnes? You're

something special,' Sam's sarcasm and clenched fists reveal his sense of betrayal at Nikki's duplicity.

John opens the questioning, 'OK Sam, where were you on Thursday evening and that night?'

'I was at the digs where you found me, Tessa from Telford!' he grimaces, crushing the paper cup.

'Who is this Tessa from Telford?' inquires John.

'Never mind, John.' Looking at Sam, Nikki continues, 'Please tell us where you were.'

'Same place, Tessa!' He drums his fingers on the desk.

'OK. Tell us about yourself, Sam,' persists Nikki.

'What do you want? I want my lawyer,' repeats Sam.

'Just tell us who you are Sam,' shouts John.

Sam brushes his greasy blonde hair away from his face, 'I'm an ex-soldier, fought in Afghanistan, separated, homeless, with one prized possession - my dog Ruby, which you know already, Tessa or DCI Barnes,' his lips droop down at the corners.

'Have you got any children?' queries John.

'Yes, two. My family lives in Shrewsbury.'

'Do you often see your children?'

His body stiffens at the remark, 'Why do you want to know?'

'A simple question to a family man,' John replies with a friendly smile.

'Is this a good cop, bad cop scenario? Which one are you, Tessa?' sniggers Sam.

'We're putting together some information, Sam. Just doing our job,' answers Nikki.

'I wish I could see my children and be near to them. If my circumstances change, I will do so,' agonises Sam.

Ayesha knocks on the door and hands a piece of paper to Nikki.

Pulling her chair closer, Nikki probes, 'You said you are ex army and fought in Afghanistan. Was it in Sangin?'

Sam squirms in his chair, 'What about Sangin?'

'Did you lose comrades in conflicts with the Taliban?'

John looks puzzled, unsure where Nikki's line of inquiry is going.

'I lost my mates,' Sam hisses.

'Are you getting any help, Sam?' quizzes John.

'I got six treatment sessions for my PTSD,' he

pauses, 'and was told to get on with life.'

'You must be pissed off then, Sam.'

'What do you think?' his eyes brim with tears.

Nikki asks again, 'Where were you on Thursday night?'

'I already told you.'

'Do you recognise Mei Wang?' Nikki pushes the photo across the table to Sam.

'Who? Who is Mei Wang?'

'So, you haven't met her?'

'No, I don't recognise who this person is and no I've never met her.'

'This is Mei Wang,' Nikki points at the photograph.

'Never seen her!' replies an expressionless Sam.

Nikki knew of the training which special ops soldiers undergo including SERE - Survival, Evasion, Resistance and Escape. A strategy to use in the event of being captured. Sam would not crack that easily.

She challenges him again, 'Have you ever been to the Lickey Hills?'

Straight faced, he answers, 'No, what is it?'

'It's a country park in south Birmingham. Have you ever been there?'

'No.'

'So how come your phone signals were located at the Lickey Hills on Thursday night?'

'I don't know. Someone must have taken my phone,' his mouth is set in a grim line, jaw tense.

'And they returned it?' a cynical John retorts.

'It's possible. People do many odd things in the shelters,' Sam sniggers.

'How come we found Ruby's excrement in the Lickey Hills?' Nikki confronts him with an unrelenting stare.

'You're kidding me. Dog shit is the same everywhere. You can't pin it on my dog,' protests Sam.

Anger swelling up in him, John asks, 'Did you kill Mei Wang?'

'I don't know who she is and no, I didn't kill her,' a confident Sam replies.

Nikki is aware that he won't crack, 'Do you want to think it over Sam?'

'Why? There's nothing to think about!''

'How do you explain the fact that your arrears to the

Child Support Agency were cleared on Friday?' John clenches his fists.

'Oh, that? I was lucky with a scratch card and I paid off my debt,' he gives a dismissive wave of his hand.

'Where did you buy the card?'

'Why?'

'So we can find out if you are telling the truth,' John strokes his stubble.

'Am I under arrest?'

'No. You're helping us with our enquiries.'

'This doesn't seem like an enquiry. It's more like a direct attack on me!' He crosses his arms.

Nikki ignores his obstinate pose, 'We need to find out a few things about you, Sam.'

'Like what?'

'Where did the money come from, why was your dog's poo found in the Lickeys and how come your phone signal can be placed at the scene of the crime.'

'I want to speak to my lawyer,' blurts Sam.

'Sure. Make a phone call and we will begin then,' agrees John.

As he is being escorted to the cells, Nikki shouts, 'is

that tattoo on your arm from the Sangin Specials?'

Sam shrugs.

27

In the police cafeteria, Nikki is eating chicken salad whilst Ayesha is tucking into her homemade prawn curry and rice. The smell of her curry is overpowering. Nikki notices a young police officer sitting at the next table is wrinkling his nose.

'My god. That smell is biting,' Nikki smiles and tucks into her lunch.

'You mean it stinks?'

'No, Ayesha, it smells divine, can I have some?' At that moment, John makes an entry with his cheese sandwich.

'Nikki, do you remember me telling you about Hamid entering the Dawal award scheme?'

'What's the Dawal award scheme?' pipes up John.

'A rich Indian donor started the scheme. It's like the Duke of Edinburgh award, but designed to encourage less able people to take part.'

'Yes, I remember him undergoing the volunteering, physical and skills sections.' Nikki observes, halfway through her sandwich.

'Wow. You remember!'

'He's my godson. How could I forget?'

'He's away for two nights doing his expedition section.'

'Home alone then?' chuckles John.

'Yes,' Ayesha looks at Nikki, 'fancy coming for a girly night out?'

'What? A Bollywood movie, more curry and reek tomorrow?' guffaws Nikki.

'Can I join you?' John pleads.

'Sure, John. I'll message you time and place,' says Ayesha, dark eyes flickering.

'We're seeing Han Li after lunch,' Nikki reminds him.

Han Li is seated in the interview room next to Sharon Rodriguez, a forty-something lawyer, with an aristocratic nose, sensual lips and a delicate chiselled face framed by bouncy blonde hair. She's elegantly turned out in an expensive suit.

After introductions, Nikki begins, 'How well did you know Mei Wang?'

'Who?' jumps in Rodriguez.

'You're too quick madam,' responds John.

Han replies with a deadpan expression, 'She was my

son's girlfriend.'

'Are you sure about that, Mr Li?'

'What are you saying, detective?' protests Rodriguez.

'You know her more intimately than simply as your son's girlfriend, don't you?'

'This is harassment and we're leaving. Come on Mr Li,' she stands up.

'Please sit down,' Nikki snarls, 'Watch this video clip and revise your statement, Mr Li.'

After watching the video, Li drops his head and mutters, 'Yes, I had sexual relations with her and I paid her money.'

'Did she blackmail you?'

'Yes!'

'Did you threaten to kill her?'

'May have done so, but I didn't mean it.'

'Did you have sex with Mei Wang sometime on Thursday?' Nikki asks.

'Yes, around 10:00 a.m. and then I went to my office.'

'Did you have protected or unprotected sex?'

'This is too personal. You need not answer this Mr Li,' interjects Rodriguez.

'I used a condom and left it in the bin!'

'Where were you between 10:00 p.m. and 5:00 a.m. Mr Li?'

'I was with a friend.'

'Can he give you an alibi?'

'No.'

'Why?'

'She's married,' he shoots a glance at Sharon Rodriguez.

Quick to grasp his drift, Nikki turns to Sharon, 'Was Mr Li with you all night?'

Shocked by being put on the spot, Sharon mumbles, 'Yes. We were in a business meeting.'

'All night?' jokes John.

'Yes.'

Nikki gets a text which confirms the triangulation shows that Han Li's phone was stationary in Edgbaston that night.

'Where do you live, Miss Rodriguez?' prods Nikki.

'Farquhar Road, Edgbaston,' pride oozing from every pore.

'One last question, Mr Li,' interjects Nikki.

Li looks up, 'What is it?'

'Did you kill her?'

'No, I didn't kill her. I liked her very much,' his body falls slack in the chair, arms hanging limply at his side, his frame shakes with convulsive sobs.

28

Nikki starts her eight-mile bike journey to Ayesha's house, which could take her up to forty minutes because of heavy traffic. She goes past Croftdown Road and onto Augustus Road, an inner city area comprising mainly of flats let to students and poor suburban housing. She passes Somali ladies pushing their prams, chatting on smartphones tucked inside their headgear, a kind of hands free device!

The traffic is slow as she moves along Lee Bank Middleway, the site of a fatal crash which killed six people a few years ago. After a slow crawl along the busy Coventry Road, she reaches Alum Rock. She smiles to herself as it brings to mind the Brummie rhyming slang "pull up your Alum Rocks" meaning pull up your socks.

She takes in the sun-faded striped fabric strung above rickety wooden stalls erected in front of the shops. Women in Muslim garb pick over the fresh vegetables, hundreds of passers by browse for bargains, others sit in a Somali restaurant sipping tea. The changing demographic of the area is palpable in the steam rising from cooking pots and smell of fresh Balti dishes.

She arrives at Ayesha's spacious four-bedroom semi in Alum Rock, a Muslim neighbourhood of Birmingham. Ayesha loves her roomy kitchen-diner and during summer enjoys sipping a soft drink on the patio, admiring her well-kept garden.

John rolls up moments later and after a couple of drinks they sit down for dinner.

Ayesha lives up to her reputation as a good cook having prepared Baigan Bharta, a dish of fried aubergines, chicken tikka masala, daal and rice.

John is quick to compliment Ayesha, 'You're such a good cook!'

'Thanks, John. Would you like to take some home for your girl friend?' Ayesha catches Nikki's eye and winks.

'I would love that and I'm sure Tina will be delighted!'

John bids them goodnight and leaves Ayesha and Nikki to unwind.

'Isn't he good looking?'

'Yes. Do you fancy him, Ayesha? You know he's engaged to a trainee journalist?'

'Well, can't I admire a handsome man?'

'You're allowed, but be careful.'

'I won't fall in love if that's what you mean!'

'No. I didn't mean it that way. Let's watch a Bollywood film.'

Ayesha logs into Netflix and they click on Devdas which stars her favourite actor, Shah Rukh Khan. His character becomes an alcoholic when his plan to marry his childhood sweetheart is thwarted.

Halfway through the film, Ayesha notices that Nikki is asleep. She makes her comfortable in the spare bedroom.

After brushing her teeth, Ayesha tosses and turns, worried that she hasn't received a message from her son, Hamid.

She hears noises from the room next door. Nikki is ranting in her sleep.

'No. Please don't give me that injection. No. Please don't let me go to sleep.'

'Where's my brother? What are you doing to him?'

'What are you doing? No! Don't put that electric thing on my head.'

'Mum, where are you? Please take us away!'

Ayesha enters Nikki's room and sees her sweating,

frothing at the mouth, her hands and legs thrashing uncontrollably. She realises that Nikki is having an epileptic seizure. She opens Nikki's bag, finds the hip flask, squeezes out a few drops of the oil, which Nikki swallows and begins to come out of her nightmare.

After a few minutes, Nikki is wide awake and asks, 'Was I talking in my sleep?'

'Yes, looks like you were having nightmares, what is it all about?'

'It's hazy. I get this recurring nightmare of someone tying me down, injecting something in my arm and putting strange electric wires on my head.'

'Do you know what it means?'

'No. I want to find out what happened.'

'Did you ask your mother?'

'No. I didn't. She's got enough on her plate.'

'What about your nanny?'

'Keisha? No, I can't ask her. She's getting old and forgetful.'

'You can try!'

'I keep bumping into her son, Delroy, he's working as a security officer at a casino now.'

'You mean he's a bouncer?'

'He's the door supervisor.'

'Same thing'

'To-May-To or To-Mah-To,' and they both laugh.

'Does he know anything?'

'No. Don't worry, I'll fathom it out one day.'

29

The woman turns onto her side and coos, 'Do you still love me?'

'I do. What a silly question to ask!'

'You're a million miles away today,' she plays with his hairy chest, making smooth movements under the silk sheets.

With a glint in his eyes he replies, 'I'm never distracted when you're around, my beauty!'

Her heart flutters and big blue eyes sparkle when he continues to caress her smooth body after making love instead of simply falling asleep.

Her body twitches in response to his phone ringing, 'That's a different ring tone. Who's calling you?'

'It's work and yes, I have another phone for official business, I need to take this.'

He puts on his dressing gown and moves to the balcony of the penthouse suite.

'Hello, what can I do for you?'

The woman couldn't hear what the caller was saying, but the man continues, 'Yes, I will deliver your consignment in forty-eight hours. When am I picking up the delivery?'

'OK, wait for my call,' and as he hung up the phone it rang again.

'Hello, yes, I'm aware that your members need to settle their children's tuition fees. I'm organising it and you will be in a position to distribute the money in seventy-two hours.'

'Please come to bed, I need you.'

'I'm coming baby,' and he slides under the sheets.

The phone rings yet again, the woman complains, 'What the hell? We're supposed to be enjoying ourselves and you're busy on the phone.'

'Sorry, babe.'

The phone continues to ring. The woman snaps, 'another ring tone. How many phones have you got? Are these for different women?'

'No, these are for work.'

He responds, 'Yes, may I help you?'

'Where are you?'

'I'm coming.'

'Who was that and where are you going?' she demands, ramming her bare foot into the seat of his jeans.

'I'll be back soon. Someone needs my help.'

'Always helping others. Have you ever thought of yourself my hero?'

He finishes getting ready, plants a kiss on her upturned face and leaves the suite.

She was right. He always helped people.

A colleague described him as a modern day Robin Hood; he didn't know whether to take that as a compliment or an insult. He had struggled to break free from the legacy of childhood abuse at the hands of his stepfather, which resulted in being raised in a succession of inadequate foster homes. This left him with an all-consuming ambition to be rich, powerful and needed by all. His inability to punish his stepfather was his biggest regret, but he had compensated for it by handing out punishment to a lot of other guilty people.

30

It is 08:00 a.m. and the duty sergeant informs Nikki that Samuel Masterson's lawyer is in the waiting room.

Nikki sits with John for the interview and takes time to observe Sam's lawyer, John Fabricant. His pointed nose, sticky out ears and bushy eyebrows are engulfed by a mass of red curly hair. A whiff of expensive aftershave fails to mask the strong smell of dust and fresh paint, which assaulted Nikki's nostrils from the time she entered the station. His tweed suit, cream silk shirt and red silk tie hang limply off his flabby frame.

Brows knitted together in a scowl, Fabricant demands, 'Why is my client being held in custody? Has he been charged?'

Nikki is struck by his piercing blue eyes which seem out of sync with the rest of his body. She composes herself; 'We have detained Mr Masterson for further questioning related to the death of Miss Mei Wang.'

'My client says he was at the shelter at the time you mentioned,' he fiddles with his bracelet.

She continues, staring at him, 'We believe Mr Masterson was near the scene of the crime.'

'Where is the proof?' snarls Fabricant.

'We triangulated Mr Masterson's phone signals which place him at the scene of the crime.'

'Did you have permission to access my client's phone?'

'We can access information based on the intelligence received.'

With an unrelenting stare he insists, 'What intelligence did you find?'

'I'm not at liberty to say.'

Fabricant hunches over as if to hide his height, 'If you cannot tell us, you must release my client.'

'As you know, I can hold your client for up to 96 hours.'

He grits his teeth, 'I need to speak to my client alone.'

Nikki and John leave the interview room.

Fabricant, who wears gloves throughout the proceedings, lends Sam his pen and asks him to sign some papers. After signing, Fabricant takes the pen and file, whispers something and stands up, smoothing his tie as he looks directly at the camera on the wall.

Those piercing blue eyes!

31

It is 11:30 a.m. and the custody officer presses the panic button. The emergency is in room 34 where Samuel is being held.

At the scene, the police officer attempts CPR on a froth-covered victim.

Nikki, a trained doctor, takes over from the officer. She inserts a breathing tube and continues with CPR. After ten minutes of resuscitation, she declares Samuel Masterson dead.

She takes samples of the froth and sends it to Dr Freeman, the pathologist.

Nikki ascertains the sequence of events leading to Sam's death. He had not consumed food in the last few hours and the lawyer was his only contact.

She asks the custody officer to inform the Special Crimes Unit and the Independent Office for Police Conduct to investigate the cause of death.

After isolating the crime scene she uses antiseptic wash and instructs the other police officers to do the same.

Nikki reviews the CCTV from Sam's cell. An hour after the interview, he presses the panic button and has a series of seizures, frothing at the mouth. The next set of recordings show the attempts at resuscitation and then

Sam being pronounced dead.

John takes a deep breath, 'Guv, what happened here?'

'I think a variant of Novichok agent might have poisoned him.'

'You mean, the Novichok agent which killed the Russians in Salisbury?'

'Yes.'

'How is that possible?'

'The only person who could have brought it in was the lawyer.'

'Could we have done anything about it?'

'Yes, if we had used a drug called Atropine and intervened earlier, he might still be alive,' her lips curl in frustration.

'What can I do?'

'I'm going to the poisons unit at the local hospital with the two officers who handled Sam. While I'm away, can you look through the CCTV from the time Fabricant entered to the time he left and recordings from other nearby cameras?'

'Sure, Guv. You get checked out and we'll see you soon.'

32

The police headquarters is buzzing with regular office workers and the Special Crimes Unit team. The health and safety team had already sealed the custody area earlier.

The combination of the pungent smell of cleaning chemicals, old coffee and stale tobacco wafting from the clothes of the smokers assails Nikki as she joins her team for a briefing.

'Any news on our lawyer, Ayesha?'

'The name John Fabricant doesn't exist in the Bar Council register,'

'So, he's a fake lawyer.'

She looks across at John who is fiddling with the laptop connection to the screen. 'What about the CCTV?'

'Daniel and I have been scouring the CCTV footage. It shows Fabricant, if that is his real name, well dressed and wearing gloves entering the building, he appears to be hunchbacked.'

He pauses, 'Listen to the conversation here between the security officer and Fabricant.'

'Why are you wearing gloves?'

'I have psoriasis,' replies Fabricant.

'What's psoriasis? Is it infectious?' challenges the officer, known as Jim.

'No!' retorts Fabricant.

'Well, what is it then?'

'It's an auto-immune disease affecting the skin and you won't catch it,' Fabricant reassures him.

'I noticed in your suitcase there's a strange-looking box, what is it?'

'Oh, that is my most expensive pen which I keep in the box. Did you think it was a gun?' chuckles Fabricant.

He flashes a toothy grin as Jim lets him in to see the prisoner.

They check the footage taken during the interview again.

Nikki, wearing her doctor's hat, asks, 'Has anyone observed his facial skin?'

'What do you mean?'

'It doesn't look real,' she rocks back and forth on her heels.

Ayesha realises something is bothering her, 'Spit it out Guv!'

'I would guess that he's wearing a face mask,' clarifies Nikki.

'How can you be sure?'

'Let's put him through our facial recognition software and see if he's on our database.'

'We'll do that,' replies Ayesha.

'Continue, John.'

'We followed him from the station and…'

'Yes, John, don't wait for a drum roll!' quips Ayesha.

'Look, as he leaves the station, he straightens up but walks with a limp.'

'Did he do anything to his face?' Nikki groans.

'No, Guv, we followed the CCTV footage of him to Weaman Street, Colmore Circus Queensway and then we lost him!'

Nikki points to Dr Freeman, 'What can you say about the victim, doctor?'

The doctor adjusts his bowtie and hypothesises, 'The preliminary findings suggest that he died of pulmonary oedema, or accumulation of water on the lungs, causing him to choke.'

'Did you carry out the post-mortem yourself, doctor?'

'My colleagues from the University Hospital did it

under controlled conditions.'

'Why not you?' interrupts John.

'I only do virtual autopsies and this case required dissection of all body parts,' the doctor informs him.

Nikki adjusts her seat to focus on Ayesha, 'Any more news on Mei Wang's computer?'

'We haven't located the laptop yet, but I managed to access her accounts,' she waits.

'Did you find loads of money?' beams John.

'5200 pounds. Not much to kill for!' babbles Ayesha.

'What do we know about our dead soldier?' interrupts Nina Kowalski.

'He was active in Afghanistan in Special Forces and was discharged three years ago.'

There is a sharp intake of breath from Nina, 'Why was he discharged?'

'He got into drugs and beat up local Afghans, including the interpreters!'

Nikki adds, 'We know his wife kicked him out of the family home in Shrewsbury. Anything to add to that?'

'He had no regular friends. During the day, he would

take up his usual spot in front of a large bookstore in Birmingham with his dog and at night he used to hang around under the bridge using drugs,' narrates John.

'He used a special heroin from Sangin,' Nikki adds.

'How can you tell?' wonders Nina.

'I've worked in and around Sangin. The local opium landlord has cross-pollinated his crop with a local flower which gives it a distinct smell,' Nikki volunteers.

'Did you try it?' chuckles Daniel.

'Can't comment on that Daniel!' and as she stands up urges everyone, 'Let's cooperate with the Special Crimes Unit and get them off our backs!'

33

It is lunchtime and Ayesha watches John unwrap his tired meal deal, a BLT sandwich with a packet of crisps and a soft drink. She puts her chicken tikka masala and chapattis in the microwave, the strong smell of cumin and other spices hit John's nose. Although he feels quite nauseated, he steadies himself and blurts out, 'Wow! It smells wonderful. Is that the same curry from two days ago that I ate?'

'No. I cooked it yesterday. Would you like some?'

He tucks into his lunch and mumbles, 'No thanks. I can't digest a curry if I'm working in the afternoon.'

'Nikki, do you want some?' shouts Ayesha.

'No thanks, I'm OK,'

As they sit down, John's curiosity gets the better of him, 'Guv, you fought in Afghanistan. What was it like? What can you tell about this soldier? You commented on his tattoo.'

'I was a doctor attached to the army in Helmand,' she maintains awkward eye contact, 'I saw some unavoidable deaths and atrocities.'

'It's inevitable in a war,' John's face is contorted, acknowledging the raw pain of her experience.

Ayesha inquires, 'What is this Sangin Special you mentioned?'

Nikki looks up and spells it out, 'A group of soldiers, distressed by the death of their colleagues, formed a group called "Sangin Specials", with the aim of planning revenge.'

'Against who?'

'Army, country or Afghans, anyone who got in their way.'

'Have they succeeded?'

'I can't go into operational details, but I think so,' she shakes her head, muttering.

Nikki receives a text message:

Aunty don't tell mum.

They beat me up.

Please come and get me.

Hamid

'Ayesha, where is Hamid's camp?'

'Why?'

'Just wondered!'

'It's at Langley Farm in Egginton, a few miles from Burton upon Trent,' Ayesha narrows her eyes in faint suspicion.

'I'll be back in a bit,' Nikki responds.

Nikki rides home to her place in Court Oak, opens the garage, which she rents from her neighbour, and starts her four-wheel drive Range Rover.

She messages Hamid to find out the names of the bullies and to get ready to be discharged.

She arrives at Langley Farm in an Indian shalwar kameez and tells the receptionist, 'I have to pick up Hamid Hussain.'

'Who are you? He can't go home yet!'

'I'm his aunt. His mother had an accident.'

'Sorry to hear that. I'll get Hamid.'

Hamid mumbles a greeting from his automatic wheelchair, a grey baseball hat pulled down firmly over his face.

After completing the formalities, Nikki takes Hamid home.

While cleaning his wounds, she asks, 'Who did this?

Why?'

'You know why! They said I'm a "spasmo" and shouldn't be in this programme,' he begins to shake with sobs.

'Who?'

'Michael Greer and Nawaz Sharif. Greer is the son of our local MP and Sharif's father owns a chain of supermarkets,'

'Have you got their phone numbers?'

'One better than that, aunty. I've got their mug shots, phone numbers and addresses,' his face hard set, unblinking eyes focussed on Nikki.

'That's my boy. Don't tell mum,' Nikki allows herself a faint reassuring smile.

'I'll triangulate their phones and send you the location in a few minutes, Aunty.'

'Good. I need to go out for a while,'

Nikki dons her motorcycle gear, slips the foldable aluminium baseball bat and ski mask into the side pocket, sips some drops of cannabis oil from her hip flask and sets off. Hamid messages her that the two boys are just outside a kebab shop off Stratford Road, a fifteen-minute ride. She parks her bike in a side alley, anonymous in her ski mask, and waits until Michael and Nawaz are alone. She delivers a hard smack to their right legs, the sickening sound of bones shattering follows and loud cries of anguish fill the air.

There are no witnesses.

Her disguised voice booms from her smartphone in the darkness, 'Don't mess with people who can't fight. I will come after you and your family if you tell anyone about this. I know who you are and where you live. Next time, I will kill you all!'

Once the first tear broke free, the rest followed like a continuous stream, Michael screams, 'No, we won't tell anyone. Please, leave us alone.'

Nawaz bellows, 'Help!' then realises that impending disaster is looming right in front of him, holds his leg and sobs, 'We won't tell anyone,'

She rings for an ambulance, gives the location of the injured and rides off.

34

It was 6:00 p.m. and the Hagley Road in the south of Birmingham, with one lane coned off for road works, looked congested.

The footpaths were packed with pedestrians, business people trying to go home, shoppers from the nearby supermarket weighed down by bags, two older women pushing their shopping trolleys, students with backpacks. Young cycle riders trying to deliver hot pizzas jostled each other in the narrow bicycle lane.

Fifty-five year old Om Gulati was returning home from work on his bicycle, he was struck by how much this road had changed over the years.

He avoided dented trash cans but free-flowing crisp packets and burger wrappers became entangled in the spokes of his bicycle wheels. Om was aware of the power of the unions, which had called for yet another strike of the bin men, causing havoc in the streets of the city. The middle of the road continued to be a major litter attraction as rubbish was strewn along the highway, blown by the wind and passing traffic, not to mention the sideshow of black bin bags on the footpath from which emanated the stench of rotten food.

Om passed the 1960s office complex designed by the famous architect, John Madin. The buildings were now earmarked for demolition and would soon be replaced by four hundred apartments and a gleaming modern office block. There were credible arguments for and against this decision but in the end it was decided that the old offices needed to be replaced.

The traffic lights changed and Om pedalled past the Oratory of Saint Philip Neri, founded by John Henry Newman in 1848.

As a fan of "Lord of the Rings", Om was intrigued to discover the link between the Oratory and the literary scholar and famous novelist, JRR Tolkien. Although Tolkien was born in South Africa, his mother returned to her roots in Birmingham and Tolkien was educated there. He used much of the city and surrounding countryside as material for his later writing. Father Francis of the Oratory in Waterworks Road was a great support to the family and eventually became Tolkien's legal guardian.

Undoubtedly, Tolkien was inspired by local architecture to create the symbolic two towers in his book, "The Lord of the Rings". Residents of the area are familiar with the landmarks also known locally as the twin towers. One is the 94 feet tall hexagonal tower known as Perrott's Folly and the other is the Edgbaston Waterworks tower, just two hundred yards apart. A "trilogy" buff, Om, visited the Oratory house to find out more about Tolkien's association with it and to see the few remaining Tolkien artefacts kept there such as

Father Francis' executor's book and the large trunk that accompanied the family from South Africa.

The next familiar landmark on Om's route was the American restaurant famous for its slogan about that special day of the week. His mouth watered as he remembered eating his favourite chicken Dijon dish with his then girlfriend, now mother of his two children.

Om was forced to weave around illegally parked cars which obstructed the traffic flow, but gave the parking enforcement officer the welcome chance to issue a flurry of tickets for the parking violations.

One of the obvious changes to the Hagley Road that he noticed was how dilapidated some of the grander buildings had become. Many were shrouded in scaffolding awaiting demolition or renovation. An upmarket retirement home had sprung up on one of the building sites promising a 'first class' lifestyle. Om knew only too well the slick advertising concealed the true cost of the arrangement. His ageing neighbour, Cyril, moved into this place after his wife died.

Brigitte, Cyril's only daughter, had told Om about the 12.5% exit fee payable if they resold the flat. She realised her nest egg of £300,000 would dwindle considerably if her dad survived for ten years.

Modern day economic fragility and the relationship between a child and parent made Om think of his own family.

The traffic moved at last, Om was beginning to wonder if the urban myth was true that that the city council shut off alternate street lights to reduce electricity bills.

The whirring of a moped, which drew level with him, interrupted his musings about the Hagley Road. From the corner of his eye, he saw a man wearing a helmet try to push him to the ground.

Before he had time to react, Om had fallen onto the kerb in a dark stretch of the road where the traffic had thinned out. The motorcyclist leaned over Om who sensed an intense pain in his chest and abdomen.

Om was overcome by a surge of emotions; surprise, anxiety and worry for his family till his breathing became heavy. Only then did he realise that the moped rider had stabbed him, grabbed his phone and made off with the bag containing his laptop.

A university student with a heavy backpack was trudging towards the bus stop when he heard the weak cry for help, 'He's stabbed me, please help!'

The student tried to keep the man warm and conscious as he rang for assistance.

The victim muttered, 'I'm Om Gulati ... live on 22 Hamilton Road... my kids... my wife.'

Om Gulati died even before the ambulance arrived.

35

John tidies up his desk, scurries down the stairs to his car and joins the rush hour traffic. As soon as he arrives home, he sends a message to Tina:

Where are you?

Are you coming here tonight?

Get a takeaway

xx

After messaging, he turns on the TV to watch the local news.

The female presenter describes how a strange man in a balaclava is randomly attacking people.

She continues, 'In our studio this evening, we have the Hon Jacob Greer, MP for Hall Green, and Saba Sharif, a local businessman. Welcome.'

The camera focuses on Greer, 'Mr Greer, would you like to tell us what happened?'

'Thanks for having us here in the studio. Our sons

got beaten up and their legs broken by an unknown assailant wearing a ski mask.'

'What was the motive? Do the boys know why they were targeted?'

'No, they don't,' counters Sharif.

'I'm sure the assailant must have said something!' enquires the wide-eyed presenter.

'I will come after you and your family,' Greer answers with a flushed face.

The teenagers had obviously omitted to mention the masked person's warning - "don't mess with people who can't fight."

The presenter explains that the boys had just completed the Dawal Awards Scheme and were returning home when the attack occurred, she urges the audience to contact the police if they know anything about the incident.

The sports news follows but it's the next item, which draws John's attention:

Breaking news
A man stabbed on Hagley Road this evening.
Details are sketchy.
A moped was seen nearby.
Victim taken to the Local Hospital.

Nikki's phone erupts as she is opening the door to her flat. It's Ayesha.

'Hi, I'm just entering the flat. Is it urgent?'

'Yes, it is when someone breaks legs in the dark!' screams Ayesha.

'I don't understand. What do you mean?'

'I need to see you now!'

Nikki discerns Ayesha's barely concealed sobs at the other end of the line.

'I'll be with you in fifteen minutes.'

It takes twenty minutes for Nikki to reach Ayesha's house. The door is ajar in anticipation of her arrival. As she enters, Hamid shoots Nikki a sullen look from the corner where he is sitting.

'Since when did you become a makeup artist?' blurts Ayesha.

'I don't know what you mean!'

'Look at this excellent make up masking the bruises under his eye, arms and legs,' she pauses, 'Guess, what I found in his bag? A tube of Arnica!'

'Oh, Arnica heals bruises and injuries. Did Hamid have a fall?'

'Don't push it, Nikki,' sniffs Ayesha.

'OK. What did you want me to do? Do nothing? Be like Mahatma Gandhi and teach Hamid to practise non-violence?'

'Yes! You're his godmother. You should protect him and teach good things,' Ayesha stalks off into the kitchen.

'Don't walk away. I can't bear to see anyone I care about get hurt.'

'But you can't keep beating up people and breaking their bones!' exclaims Ayesha.

'Did you break any bones, Aunty?' Hamid asks.

'No, I didn't do that!'

'We picked it up on the news!' bellows Ayesha.

'Maybe,' Nikki looks down, avoiding their gaze.

'I pour my heart out to you and the next thing is - you try to destroy it!' Ayesha runs her hands through her hair.

'I'm so sorry, Ayesha,' looking her straight in the eyes.

'Don't ever do this again. Now we will eat.'

Nikki returns to her flat, settles down in her chair and reflects upon the caring relationship between Ayesha and Hamid. She considers how important it is to Ayesha that Hamid learns to be true to himself, honest and caring. She compares that to her own upbringing. Although her mother was a caring parent, her job necessitated her delegating the care of her children to Keisha, their nanny. Nikki wondered whether her mum truly loved them or was more interested in proving herself to be a good wife and a career woman, thus abdicating her parental responsibilities. It was all too hazy. If only she could cuddle up to her mum and talk it through. Alas, that ship had sailed.

No message from Tina. John has a beer and settles down to an evening alone.

36

As Nikki parks her bike, the duty officer comes running, 'Guv, they found another body.'

'Where?'

'Behind Devil's Den. The local bobby rang us a few minutes ago.'

'Who found the body?'

'The bartender.'

'OK, I'm leaving right now. When you see DC Williamson, send him there. Call SOCA and Dr Freeman.'

'Yes, Guv,' the officer puffs out his chest proudly. In his thirty-year career he had never seen a DCI as quick to respond as her!

Nikki arrives at Devil's Den to find the front door ajar and Ivan Popescu, the bartender; staring into space, mouth agape.

Nikki shouts, 'Ivan, are you all right?'

Ivan stands up, trembling, 'Yes, I'm OK.'

'What happened here?'

'Let me show you,' he shuffles towards the open

door.

He guides Nikki along the adjoining alley which is littered with discarded cans and food wrappers. Amongst the detritus by the bins, Nikki makes out the shape of a prone body.

She approaches without disturbing the scene and confirms that it's a woman's body. She checks for a pulse and shouts in a futile attempt to rouse the woman. No response. The body feels cold. Nikki estimates that the woman must have been dead for at least ten hours.

Nikki wears her disposable gloves to search the pockets of the dead woman. She notices that the dried blood on the back of the woman's neck must have trickled down from a head wound on the scalp.

She takes pictures of the body and the surrounding area.

They go inside to wait for the SOCO team and the pathologist.

'Ivan, was the CCTV working last night?'

'Yes, detective.'

'Show it to me, please.'

Ivan rewinds the footage from the CCTV camera sited at the rear of the building. He stops and restarts it at

8:30 p.m. There is no activity till 9:07 p.m. when a man appears, unaware he is facing the CCTV camera. It captures his face on the screen. It is 9:12 p.m. and he is still waiting when a woman wearing a skirt and blouse walks out. She is looking at her phone at the moment that the man comes from behind and hits her with a heavy metallic object. She falls to the ground. The man grabs her phone and bag, drags the body behind the bins and disappears.

Nikki asks Ivan to show her the recordings of the bar. At 8:50 p.m. an attractive tall brunette, wearing a cream blouse and black skirt, walks in and orders a drink.

Ivan places a glass of red wine in front of her. She looks at her phone whilst sipping the wine and at 9:11 p.m. she walks to the back door.

Nikki continues to look at the CCTV from 8:30 p.m. onwards. She sees nothing untoward until 9:00 p.m. when a stocky man catches her eye. He sits in a corner looking at the tall brunette. At 9:10 p.m. the man uses his phone, the brunette looks at her phone and walks to the door at 9:11 p.m.

There is no sign of the stocky man after 9.11 p.m.

Nikki asks Ivan to play the CCTV footage from the camera at the front of the club. They notice a lot of people entering the club, but at 9:17 p.m. she identifies the man who attacked the woman handing over something to another person. She zooms in and finds it is the same stocky man who is receiving something. She observes a man who might be wearing a facemask; nevertheless it does not conceal the striking feature of his steely blue eyes.

Nikki makes copies of these recordings on her USB, aware that the SOCO team will bag all the evidence on arrival.

John arrives at the scene and inquires, 'Who is it Guv?'

'Ivan found the body of a young woman.'

'Can I see?'

'Sure.'

He puts on his crime scene outer shoes and joins Nikki.

She's mystified at John's changing expressions as he approaches the body. The concentration evident in furrowed brows and narrowed eyes alter in a split second as he sees the face. He freezes, staring wide-eyed at the woman and drops to his knees. A long, low howl of raw grief reverberates around the alley.

'John, what's the matter? Do you know this woman?'

Between choking sobs he manages to murmur, 'She's my girlfriend, Tina!'

37

Nikki finds it difficult to empathise with John who had lost his loved one. She wishes that she could tell him that she suffers from a little known condition called alexithymia. The syndrome causes difficulty in recognising and expressing her own emotions and those of other people such as sadness in this instance.

Whilst watching Bollywood movies with Ayesha, Nikki would be at a loss to understand why her friend was moved to tears by some scenes that she found almost comical. Over the years, she had tried to learn what emotional response was expected in certain situations, but it was not a genuine heartfelt expression of feeling. On one occasion, Ayesha had mentioned that she would love to meet a nice man and fall in love all over again. Nikki didn't understand why she wanted to do that and she herself entertained no plans to go down that path.

Nikki approaches John and tilting her head in an attempt at sympathy mumbles, 'Will you be all right, John?'

'Seriously, Guv? How can I be all right? I have just lost the woman I was going to marry!' He wipes away streams of tears.

'I understand John, you must be devastated. Why don't you go home or, better still, stay with your parents? You could do with some company,' she mutters.

'I want to find out who killed Tina and why!'

'Take a break John.'

'Don't ask me to take a break. I'm a police officer and my duty is to catch the killer.'

'I appreciate that. Perhaps you can join us later.'

'I want to be a part of the investigation. I'm not going anywhere,' shouts John.

'This is too close to your heart, John. You may not think rationally.'

'Let me be the judge of that, Guv.'

'I'm not big on counselling, John, but this is standard operating procedure.'

'I know about you, Guv. You've never followed the rules in your life, why should I?'

'I see. You must have asked your parents to open my file,' Nikki smiles ruefully.

'Something like that.'

'OK. You're still on the case, but I will handle anything about Tina. Is that a deal?'

'Yes.'

'We will find the killer or killers John,' Nikki reassures him.

38

Superintendent Bob Newton greets Nikki at the entrance to the police station.

It surprises her to see him at this early hour, 'Good morning, sir. What brings you to the station first thing in the morning?'

She notices from the corner of her eye how the staff attempt to look busy to impress the superintendent.

'Morning, Acting DCI Barnes. I had to come,' he pauses.

'I understand, sir. DC Williamson is your godson and you need to be there for him.'

'I'm glad you understand the situation,' he says massaging his temples, 'I informed his parents and they will arrive soon.'

'Will you be taking over the investigation, sir?'

'No. I won't bring in anyone from outside either. You're an accomplished officer and I know you will address the present situation effectively.'

'Thank you, sir.'

They enter the incident room where everyone has assembled. John follows Nikki and the superintendent.

Bob Newton addresses the team, 'I'm not here to

take over the investigation. I'm here to give you all my support and trust that you will apprehend the killer soon,' he pauses, looks at John, 'DC Williamson, I am sorry for your loss. Do you want to take time off?'

John adjusts his cuffs awkwardly, 'Thank you, sir, for your kind words. I've spoken to Acting DCI Barnes and I'm aware of my boundaries during this investigation.'

'Good,' looking at Nikki, 'Please carry on. I will sit and listen.'

Nikki shuffles her paperwork, looks at the group and begins, 'we have information. Tina died at 9:12 p.m. and I have an idea who the killer is.'

'Who is the killer?' Nina Kowalski, the criminal psychologist, asks.

'He's another soldier who fought in Sangin alongside Samuel Masterson.'

'What's the connection between the two murders and the soldiers who fought in Afghanistan?'

'We don't know yet,' she looks across the room at the SOCO officer and Khalid Hussain, 'Any more input?'

Khalid rubs his belly, 'No, DCI Barnes. There were no foot marks and no sign of the weapon with which they killed the victim.'

'Tina Wyatt, that is her name,' interjects John.

'I've identified the victim as Tina Wyatt, John's fiancé,' Nikki informs them.

Ayesha puts her hand on John's shoulder; Khalid Hussain shoots him a sympathetic look.

'Have you got something for us, Ayesha?' inquires Nikki.

'Yes, Guv. John gave me Tina's phone number and I downloaded the messages from the server.'

'I thought you need permission from the mobile carriers concerned,' a wide-eyed Bob Newton objects.

'We can download it with software which Ayesha has developed.'

'Is it permissible as evidence in court?'

'The messages give us an idea of the character, allow us to develop a storyline and look for definitive clues, and no, sir, we will not submit it to the public prosecutor,' Nikki adds.

'Thank God for that!' he retorts, shuffling in his chair.

Ayesha, with a glance of affection at John, begins, 'This will be uncomfortable for you. Do you want to leave?'

'No. I'm a professional police officer and I can take bad news,' John lifts up his head.

'I have divided Tina's messages into four groups: John, Tina's mother, a journalist called Julian Pettifer and Om Gulati.'

She smiles at John with reassurance like balm, 'There are private messages between John and Tina.'

John smiles and Ayesha continues, 'there was a different dialogue with her mother regarding imminent marriage. She didn't want to marry John.' Ayesha, wiping her eyes, turns to him with a pitying apologetic grimace.

John gives a fake smile, 'Continue, Ayesha, I'm OK. I was aware something was not right.'

Ayesha focuses on Julian Pettifer.

'Julian Pettifer is an award winning investigative journalist based in Birmingham,' she pauses.

'Yes, continue,' Nikki encourages.

'Julian is married with two children,' she almost chokes on the words, 'Tina was having an affair with him,' and her voice trails off.

'Do you want to continue or shall I take over?' Nikki's impatience is obvious.

Ayesha composes herself, 'in the last few weeks,

there have been angry messages between the two. Tina wanted Julian Pettifer to leave his wife, he would not make a commitment, she wanted to tell his wife.'

John sags against the wall, 'Where did it end up, this blackmail?'

'Pettifer stopped answering her calls three days ago. I have triangulated his phone, he seems to be in Devon.'

'Is anyone safe from you, Ayesha?' Nina tries to lighten the atmosphere.

'The fourth person is Om Gulati, the finance director of Metro University,' Ayesha stands up to ease her aching muscles.

'What is his role?' Bob Newton interjects.

'Om Gulati was trying to get hold of Julian Pettifer who had gone AWOL. He contacted Tina to ask her to forward to Pettifer the tip that something big would happen soon. Tina then convinced Om to give her the information about Metro University.'

'How did it finish?' Nina interrupts.

'Tina mentions that she knows of the scandal, but wants to know more about it.'

The last message from Om Gulati to Tina is:

Hi, Om here

Come to Devil's Den at 8:30 p.m.

Will give you more details.

Nikki wraps up the meeting, 'Thank you, Ayesha, for getting this information so fast. We will find the soldier under the bridge. One of you find out the whereabouts of Om Gulati. Come on, John.'

As they are about to leave the room, Nikki wonders if she should put her arm around John to show her sympathy, but she realises that it might seem inappropriate since she is his boss. If only she didn't feel so awkward at expressing emotion, she felt as out of place as a pepperoni that had made its way onto a vegetarian pizza!

At that moment, the duty officer enters the incident room, flushed and breathless, 'The person who was mugged and killed last night was Om Gulati!'

39

The burner phone rings, the blue-eyed man snatches it from the table.

The caller speaks in Pashto, 'Salaam Walekum Saab,'

'Walekum Salaam,' he gives the traditional response but is unable to disguise the stress in his tone of voice, 'Why are you ringing me now?' he continues.

'Send that money right away,' growls the caller.

'I'm doing my best, but there is a shortfall. I'll send it soon,' pleads the man.

'I am not bothered about your problems. If I don't get it by tomorrow, I will divert the delivery to the Turks in London.'

'Please don't. I will transfer the money.'

'Use the "hawala" method if you don't have immediate cash to send. You are cutting it fine,' the Afghani hisses.

The blue-eyed man had made "hawala" transfers in the past through his friend, Syed Quddus, until Syed was shot dead by competitors in Sangin three months ago.

Syed Quddus, an American soldier who converted to Islam, decided to remain in Afghanistan to take over the business of an ailing Afghan drug lord. It wasn't long before the lord's third wife found herself widowed and Syed married her soon after.

Syed Quddus and the blue-eyed man undertook the traditional "hawala", in which they transferred money via a network of hawala brokers, or hawaladars. It was "money transfer without money movement", based on the honesty system taking place outside of the conventional banking system.

He makes himself a coffee and recollects how he used soldiers, returning home from duty in Sangin, to smuggle bags of heroin. They would rendezvous with him outside a UK military airfield, content to hand over the contraband in return for a generous commission for their trouble knowing that the drugs would be refined and sold on for a massive profit.

Once, the drug smuggling operation was almost compromised by a tip-off to a journalist, but the journalist's scoop died with him in a road traffic accident.

An alternative route became necessary when the number of soldiers returning from Afghanistan slowed to a trickle. It was then that he contacted Azami Khan, the drug lord of Helmand, a region that grew ninety percent of the world's supply of heroin. Drug trafficking from Afghanistan into Iran, Turkey and Eastern Europe was effortless thanks to the easily bribed officials in the army and police force of the countries en route. Drugs were ingeniously concealed in fire extinguishers, marble statues and even cases of baklava! From there the drugs entered Greece, Albania, Kosovo and Serbia.

He had a friend in Kosovo, Egzon Gashi, who ensured that the drugs arrived in the UK. Most of the drugs sold in the UK were destined for private users who bought in bulk for private parties in the rich neighbourhoods. They sold the leftovers on the streets as social welfare!

He notices an incoming message on the phone:

Call me now

Egzon

He rings Egzon Gashi in Kosovo, 'what is it? Why this urgency?'

Egzon is agitated, 'You shouldn't have used the cat food!'

"Cat food" was another name for the nerve agent, similar to Novichok, which was used in the Salisbury poisonings.

'I had no choice,' he explains.

'You compromised us all,' shouts Egzon.

'Look mate. I had to make a quick decision.'

'You could have used a different method,' argues

Egzon.

'I had no time,' he snarls.

'We both need to answer to my boss. It will expose him if the national intelligence finds out the origin of the agent,' mutters Egzon.

'We will deal with that if it happens,' concludes the blue-eyed man.

40

As they are going down the steps, Nikki turns to John, 'we can't take your car on the High Street as it's pedestrianised. Let me go on my bike and if I find him, I'll call for help to pick him up.'

'You're bypassing me,' protests John.

'No, I'm being realistic.'

'Ok, I'll wait for you,' John reluctantly agrees.

Nikki heads southwest from Steely Lane onto Colmore Circus and then to High Street via Temple Row, she notices several shops are still closed and stops in front of the bookstore.

Three homeless people have chosen their pitch in front of the shop and are busy arranging their worldly goods, ready to beg. The man she wants is not there.

She shows them a picture of the killer. The first two people have no idea who he is. The third person, an anorexic heroin addict, looks fifty-something but in reality might only be in her thirties. The drug had stolen the sunshine from her life; she looks like she is locked in a cage of fear.

'Hi, I'm Nikki. Where can I find this man?'

'Are you a pig?'

'Yes, if you say so. I'm Detective Inspector Barnes,' looking at her in pained anticipation.

'Got any heroin?'

'It's early, don't you think?'

'What do you care?'

'I haven't got any heroin, but I'll give you some money. Why don't you get cleaned up?'

'Since when do they pay you to be a social worker too?' chuckles the woman.

'OK. You have a point,' Nikki hands over a ten pound note, 'Can you tell me about him? Where might he be now?'

The woman snatches the banknote, shoves it inside her bra and looks up, 'His name is Ezekial, I think. We call him Ezi the strong man because he kicks the shit out of people who want to attack us.'

'Has he got a record?'

'Not that I know of. He's an ex-soldier. Fought in Afghanistan, became a heroin addict, lost everything and he landed up here from Hereford,' she offers, rocking from side to side.

'Where is he today?'

'Dunno, but tonight, when the shops shut, he'll be

under the Hockley Bridge.'

'Thanks. What's your name?'

'You don't need to know. I'm not a criminal,' the woman mutters, closing her eyes.

Nikki asks John and Ayesha to meet her in the office for a brainstorming session.

'I called you in to talk about something off the record.'

'Are we hacking into someone's accounts?' Ayesha chuckles.

'Yes,' Nikki confesses.

'Are we allowed to do it? Is it admissible in court?' John inquires.

'You're just like Nina Kowalski,' Ayesha grumbles.

'What do you mean?'

'Asking about legality!'

'We'll do the ground work and bring in the right suspects for questioning,' Nikki clarifies.

'OK. Whose account do I need to hack, boss?'

'I want you to carry out a quick forensic accounting

of Metro University's accounts and see if there is any untoward activity.'

'How far back do you want me to go?'

'Look for large deposits and withdrawals made over the last two years.'

'What about transfers to accounts which are outside the UK?' interrupts John.

'Well done, Sherlock!' Ayesha winks.

'Keep this to yourself. Come back to me ASAP,' Nikki instructs Ayesha.

Ayesha sits in front of her computer with a cup of coffee and hacks into the accounts of Metro University.

Her first task is to find out who is depositing illegal funds into the university's account. She quickly identifies the company responsible.

Ayesha looks at the layering phase of money laundering, where certain individuals take advantage of legitimate financial mechanisms to hide the source of their funds.

She finds two shell corporations, which lack real assets and business activity, which were set up to hold and move illicit funds.

Finally, Ayesha discovers how they have been converting the illicit funds into a legitimate form.

After two hours, a loud thump of her fist on the desk signals that she has successfully completed her task. She beams with satisfaction.

41

Ayesha pours herself a mug of coffee and looks up as Nikki and John enter the room deep in conversation.

'I didn't think you would be back so soon!' exclaims Ayesha.

'We need to go back to Hockley to see the soldier this evening,' observes Nikki.

'Why do you think so many soldiers are homeless, Nikki?' mutters Ayesha.

'It's a sad situation, Ayesha. 13,000 veterans are homeless and they sleep in doorways, bus stops and parks.'

'How do you think they're coping?'

'A well informed source has told me that almost all of these ex-soldiers are struggling with the devastating effects of PTSD.'

'That must be common,' comments John.

'Yes, it's true. Soldiers have nightmares in which they see the faces of the men they have killed and wake up screaming, soaked in sweat,' Nikki continues, 'Those suffering from PTSD sometimes seek relief in drugs and alcohol, then they become hooked. This impacts their marriage and in a short time the veteran can find himself separated and homeless.'

John looks anguished, 'The government should do more for the soldiers.'

'The government has an on-going duty of care as mentioned in the Armed Forces Covenant.'

'What does the covenant say?'

'It states that veterans should have priority status in applying for government sponsored affordable housing schemes,' Nikki pauses, 'and support should be available for all service personnel to assist their transition from service to civilian life.'

'You did well in civvy street, boss!' chuckles John.

Ayesha probes, 'By "civvy street" are you referring to civilian life with a career or job after discharge from the armed forces?'

'Wow. You have an answer for everything, Ayesha!' John raises his right eyebrow.

'Ayesha came first in her class and remembers everything written in small print!' laughs Nikki.

'Guv, you've settled into civvy street very well,' John congratulates her.

'I was lucky,' Nikki muses.

The conversation prompts Nikki to reflect on her own transition to civilian life. Long before Nikki Barnes joined the police force, she enlisted in the army while she was studying medicine and rose to the rank of major after she qualified as a surgeon. On her second tour of Afghanistan, she entered the Sangin theatre, which is also an important trading centre for opium. Of the many gruesome events in the field, one sticks out in her mind in which twenty-five soldiers died and ten others were badly injured in an operation to rescue a warlord's son. Nikki had to do minor surgery on the walking wounded in the field and flew with the seriously injured to operate on their penetrating traumas.

Nikki recollected the living conditions of the inhabitants of the region in scattered isolated hamlets. The most common form of housing was a multi-storey fortified farm with high walls built from a mixture of sand and straw.

A group of soldiers were ordered to attach bar mines to the walls of one of these farms, which the Taliban were using as cover to attack the army compound. The intention was to detonate the mines, blowing holes in the walls to expose the Taliban and reduce the chances of them mounting successful attacks from the cover of the walls. Whilst the soldiers were attempting to attach the mines, the Taliban attacked from all sides and shot many of the soldier's dead. Four Taliban fighters advanced and saw Nikki compressing the chest wound of a critically injured soldier.

One of the soldiers spoke in Pashto to the others, 'Woman soldier here. Let us enjoy and then kill her.'

Nikki understood what the Taliban soldier had said and got ready. She shoved a big cotton ball in the wounded soldier's chest to prevent further blood loss and said, 'I'll be back soon mate, I promise.'

The Taliban circled around her, singing a tribal song to celebrate her body. One came forward, toting his machine gun. Nikki disarmed the Taliban of his gun and shot dead the other three with it. She then turned her attention to the startled first Taliban and in one fell swoop strangled him. She returned to tend to the injured soldier until reinforcements arrived and took away the soldier and Nikki.

Nikki operated on his bleeding spleen. Once he became stable, she transferred the injured soldier to the military hospital in Birmingham. From that day, Major Nikki Barnes became a part of the folklore of British soldiers.

Ayesha disturbs her reverie, 'I have more information from Tina's phone.'

'John, is it all right if we discuss this while you're present?' Nikki inquires.

'Yes, Guv.'

'There are some exchanges between Tina and her girl friend Julie,' Ayesha reads:

I love Julian

Can't live without him

Not sure he wants me

Is it infatuation on my part?

Does he only want me for my body?

So many questions!

Nikki and John listen in stunned silence. Ayesha stutters as she reads Julie's reply:

You're wrong.

Julian is married, self-centred.

He won't leave his wife and kids.

You're just a game for him.

Tell John, he will forgive you.

Forget Julian.

John grabs a chair and punches it hard. Ayesha reaches out with trembling hands to embrace him.

Nikki witnesses the emotional scene without comment. Allowing John a few moments to compose himself, she opens the door, 'John, we need to go now.' Nikki turns to Ayesha, 'Go deep into the Metro University accounts and bring in Han Li tomorrow morning for questioning.'

42

Nikki and John arrive at Hockley Bridge to search for the soldier in the unofficial camp for the homeless. John steps gingerly over the pools of muddy water, beer cans and black bin bags to avoid spoiling his trousers and shoes. Nikki is familiar with the surroundings so warns him to look out for faeces and animals roaming around. An unknown graffiti artist had vandalised a plastic toilet donated by a charity. As they come to the bottom of the steps, Nikki spots Tony, the homeless man she had met before. He is shouting, 'Nate, wake up, man. What's going on? Wake up!'

Nikki is alarmed to see that Nate is convulsing, froth streaming out of his mouth and then he stops breathing. She grabs a pre-loaded syringe of Narcan from her bag and quickly injects it into Nate's neck vein. As he begins to regain consciousness, Nikki asks him and Tony what happened.

Tony's throat tightens with emotion, 'There was a bloke here an hour ago handing out a free supply of heroin.'

'Did he give it to all of you?' John asks.

'Yes, but I didn't take it,' Tony sinks to his knees on the steps.

'You saved my life. You're not an addict. Who are you?' Nate asks Nikki in a hoarse whisper.

'I'll explain later. Do you think other people here have injected themselves?'

'Sure. Who would pass up a free gift? No one is stupid enough to wait!' Nate mumbles.

'Except me,' Tony grunts.

'What did you give Nate?' John asks.

'Narcan, also known as Naloxone, which reverses the respiratory depression caused by drugs like heroin and fentanyl,' Nikki explains.

'Do you always carry Narcan?'

'Yes, it's a sign of the times, John. We should always carry it to save lives. Follow me.' She sprints towards the inner lair of the camp.

They find people lying on the ground in various stages of coma. Realising the gravity of the situation, Nikki rings the emergency services and instructs the ambulance personnel to bring enough supplies of Narcan.

'I hope we're not too late, John,' Nikki stutters and walks towards the soldier they want to question.

He's lying on the ground, unconscious, not breathing. Nikki feels for his pulse and attempts to resuscitate him, she continues until the ambulance team arrives and takes over from her, but their efforts are in vain. The soldier is dead along with seven other homeless addicts.

John is visibly shaken. 'What happened here, Guv?'

'Someone has played a cunning game. All these people took heroin laced with fentanyl, which lead to quick deaths. That's why we only managed to save one person,' Nikki's lip curls in disgust.

'Were they all given a cheap, inferior drug?'

'Yes, John. It had been set up to appear as if everyone took the same drug, with the main target being our soldier,' mutters Nikki.

'Why did the perpetrator mix the drugs?'

Heroin is expensive. Our main suspect mixed heroin with cheap synthetic fentanyl.'

'Isn't fentanyl an anaesthetic pain killer?'

'Bang on. Fentanyl, when injected, can depress breathing and cause immediate death.'

Nikki goes back to Nate and Tony.

'Can you describe the person who gave you the drug?'

'It was getting dark so I couldn't make out his clothes, but….'

'But, what?' John insists.

'He had deep blue piercing eyes!'

43

Superintendent Bob Newton, flanked by Deidre Watson the Police and Crime Commissioner and the investigative team, addresses a packed press conference. After introducing the team to the press, Bob Newton begins, 'I intend to read out a short statement of the facts as we know them so far. My colleague, Professor Cooper, will do the same and then we will answer a few questions.'

He nods at Deidre who is pouting, sitting with arms crossed, attempting a fake smile.

He continues, 'We were called to the Hockley bridge area today by our Acting DCI. Eight homeless people lived there and all of them took a lethal concoction of drugs. Seven of them were pronounced dead by ambulance staff at the scene. Our officer saved a man from respiratory arrest before the ambulance team arrived. He was taken to a local hospital.'

Newton sips some water and continues, 'He is doing well. Our thoughts go out to the family of the deceased and police officers are investigating the circumstances leading to these horrific deaths.'

Deidre yawns and reaches for a glass of water.

Newton's annoyance at Deidre's non-verbal gestures is palpable, 'Can I remind all of you to respect the deceased in reporting this disturbing story and if you have any information, to contact us.'

He signals to Dr Ken Cooper to make his statement. The fifty something, greying doctor looks dapper in his sports jacket, open-neck shirt and jeans, he adjusts his glasses and reads, 'Blood analysis from the victim in hospital reveals a high concentration of fentanyl, a strong analgesic used in anaesthesia, mixed with heroin.'

Peering at the assembly over his reading glasses, he continues, 'He survived because he had a single shot of Narcan which reverses the respiratory depression caused by these drugs. Narcan is short acting and so the ambulance staff gave him another shot en route to A & E.'

Newton gives an encouraging nod as Dr Cooper draws to a close, 'We continue to monitor this gentleman and have given him a further infusion of Narcan to reverse the effects of the heroin and fentanyl.'

It is Deidre Watson's turn, 'I am of the firm opinion that Class A drugs should be decriminalised and the policy of outright prohibition must be changed.'

This is a bolt from the blue to Bob Newton who doesn't see eye to eye on policing issues with Deidre. Typical of her to ignore the personal tragedy of the casualties and address the press conference with her political angle on drugs, underfunding and decreasing police numbers.

Bob purses his lips, his irritation clear, 'Well, ladies and gentlemen, any questions?'

A local newspaper reporter raises his hand, 'What do you think happened here?'

'It's too early to speculate, but we know the deceased took a rogue batch of heroin cut with fentanyl.'

A woman in a blue suit, the local TV correspondent, asks, 'Do we know who sold this drug?'

'No. We are pursuing all avenues to find out what happened here.'

National TV news correspondents had already homed in on the story, a grey suited, serious correspondent pushed for more details, 'You mentioned a police officer administered a life saving dose of Narcan. Who was that officer?'

'Our DCI Barnes who was following a lead and happened to be near the scene.'

'Why didn't DCI Barnes save the others?'

'It isn't routine practice for officers to carry Narcan, but, luckily for this man, on this occasion DCI Barnes had just enough with her to save him.'

'Who is this DCI Barnes? Why was she near the scene? Has it got anything to do with the killings of two women and the death of a prisoner in custody?' a plump middle-aged journalist thrusts his microphone at Bob.

'DCI Barnes has been investigating the murders which have shocked the community.'

Deidre chimes in, 'We have a shortage of police officers because of budget cuts. I noticed that despite her limited experience, DI Barnes has been designated Acting DCI,' she complains.

'Is that true, Superintendent?' the plump journalist challenges.

'This is neither the time nor the place to talk about the staffing of the force. We are adjusting to temporary personnel changes and Acting DCI Barnes is efficient and ready for the task,' Bob booms.

He turns to Professor Cooper, 'I'm sure you will come up with more information, which will assist us with our investigations.'

As someone at the back raises his hand, Bob brings the meeting to a conclusion, 'We have a lot of questions to answer and will come back to you as soon as we have more information, goodnight.'

The journalists are hungry for answers, but Bob firmly closes down further questions. The plump guy notices Bob usher Deidre to the back door forestalling further awkward statements.

The man with the piercing blue eyes is closely following the televised police press conference and vows to himself, 'Need to get rid of DCI Barnes!'

44

Bob Newton grabs Nikki, 'Barnes, I'm bringing in detectives from Scotland Yard.'

'Why, sir?' John inquires.

Bob snaps, 'You want to know why? Deidre Watson made me look like a fool with her political speech and questioning my judgement in trusting your rookie boss, DI Barnes!'

'I'm sorry, sir. If you wish to bring in other officers from the Yard, I'll willingly work under them,' Nikki answers.

'No, sir. You can't bring in an outsider. DCI Barnes is doing her best!' John insists.

'The public and the press want answers and I want to wrap this up!' persists Newton.

'Uncle, don't do this!' John pleads. 'We are so close to catching the killer.'

John had always called Bob Newton and DCI Hill, "uncle" when he was growing up and these people had the same affection for him.

Bob smiles, 'you have come a long way, son. OK, DCI Barnes, you've got a week.'

'No, uncle, two weeks!'

'Are you haggling with me, John? OK, I approve one week. Now get on with it.'

John hugs Bob, against protocol, 'Thanks, Uncle.'

Nikki gathers the team together and asks Nina Kowalski, 'What do you make of these killings and the psyche of the killer?'

Nina looks up from her notes, 'I don't think the killer is a monster!'

'What? Not a monster?' quips John.

'Listen. This person needs help. We need to understand what moral dilemmas this person has faced on the way to committing these crimes.'

'Enough of this psychobabble,' shouts Daniel Aboah.

'Daniel, why don't you check more footage around the Hockley area?' Nikki commands.

'OK. Guv,' Daniels sulks and walks out of the room.

'Continue Nina.'

Nina sips some water, 'The killer has a twisted logic in the horrible things he is doing. It should help us if we understand the backstory lurking in the killer's psychology.'

'Are you able to paint this picture yet?' Ayesha queries.

'Not completely. This person is driven by a history of past trauma, either childhood abuse or domestic violence.'

'I read about this at Hendon, but could you put this in context here?' John asks.

'A simple analogy would be a dog bite. No one would find fault with a forty-year-old man who walks with a limp and hates dogs because a Rotweiller bit him when he was five years old. We have to understand why the violence happens and why the killer does it.'

'Can we assume that the killer is intelligent?' Nikki probes.

Nina is in her element, 'Let me indulge in explaining the organised and disorganised typology of serial killers. Our killer seems to be organised, with above average intelligence, skilled, employed and able.'

'How can you label him with such accuracy?' John contends.

'You have a serial killer who has left no finger prints or blood in a planned attack in the custody cell and the mass killing by drug overdose in Hockley.'

'So he plans these killings?' Ayesha mutters.

'Yes. He was also meticulous in organising the killings of Mei and Tina when he erased the links of the killers to himself.'

'Think of Om Gulati's murder,' Nikki adds.

'He took on the role of a moped mugger and achieved his goal without being seen.'

'Or could he be someone else?' John asks.

'It's possible.'

'What kind of person are we dealing with?' Nikki ponders.

'This serial killer has a cluster type B personality, as assessed using the diagnostic and statistical manual, which means he is a sociopath or psychopath. He is unstable, self-centred and prone to being manipulative. Does he regret killing others? We don't know yet,' Nina concludes.

'Thanks, Nina. Anymore news, Ayesha?'

'I found out about the money laundering.'

'Don't keep us in suspense,' John beams.

'The accounts of Metro University are accessed by more than two authorised signatories. There is a footprint of a third person who has also been accessing the account.'

'Did you get permission to access these accounts? And...' Nina raises her eyebrow.

'Time is running out,' Nikki swiftly cuts her off. 'Let's move on.'

'I didn't get an answer!'

'This discussion is on a need-to-know basis, let's not interrupt Ayesha,' Nikki doesn't want others to know Ayesha hacked into the Metro University accounts.

'Every three months they deposit a large amount of money in the Metro account and a few days later it gets distributed.'

'What sums are we talking about here?' John asks.

'We're talking of up to twenty-five million pounds, then the sums decrease until they deposit another large sum.'

'Do we know the source of the deposits?'

'It comes from a subsidiary company belonging to Han Li.'

'How does it work?' Nina asks.

Nikki nods and Ayesha continues, 'Cash is saved every day in Han Li's subsidiary company's account at various branches of the famous Neutrone Bank. They then move this to the accounts of Metro University.'

'So, cash generated by illegal means is invested in Neutrone Bank?' John asks.

'It looks like it. They're laundering the money according to the cookbook,' Ayesha chuckles.

John leans forward, 'Ayesha, how does this cookbook work?'

'Dirty money is mixed in the bank and from there it gets layered and, before you ask,' Ayesha smiles at John, 'layering means they move this money to the bank account of company x, which in this case is the Metro University. From here they channel the money to three different avenues.'

Nina interjects, 'Who is receiving this money?'

'A part of the money is wire transferred to two off shore accounts in the Cayman Islands, a loan to a company in the Channel Islands and payment of false invoices generated by Metro University.'

'Quite a complex procedure,' John says.

'The third angle is to buy properties to integrate laundered money back into the economy making the money legitimate,' Ayesha concludes.

'We could see how Han Li has expanded his legit empire when we walked around his supermarket,' John confirms.

'How much do you think Metro University made last year?' Nikki asks.

'Forty million pounds,' Ayesha explains.

'I can't see student fees accounting for such large sums deposited!' John says.

'You're right, Ayesha agrees. 'It's very fishy!'

'We need to find out Om Gulati's role in this affair,' John adds.

'Om Gulati wanted to talk to Tina about the scandal and perhaps spoke at length to Julian Pettifer. I think he was a genuine whistleblower, but, Ayesha, look at his accounts,' adds Nikki.

Nina explodes, 'I'm not happy. You're being unethical and are hacking into people's accounts without their permission.'

Nikki ignores her, 'Let's pull in Han Li and Timothy Robinson, the CEO of Metro University for questioning.'

45

Han Li and his lawyer, Sharon Rodriguez, are engaged in an intimate discussion in the interview room when Nikki arrives. She coughs to get their attention and pulls up a stool, 'Hello, Mr Li. Would you like to tell me about your connection with the Metro University?'

Han Li looks surprised, 'Should I know about the University?'

'Yes, you should,' quips John as he enters the room.

'Oh yes, I think Mei Wang attended the university,' he looks at his lawyer for support.

'Are you sure, Mr Li?' John challenges him. 'Is that the only connection?'

'Come out with straight questions constable. We don't like innuendos', explodes Rodriguez.

'Let me be clear then. Have you any financial dealings with Metro University?' Nikki asks.

Han Li lifts his head and looks her straight in the eye, 'No, I don't.'

Pushing documents towards Han Li, Nikki says, 'Look at this and explain.'

Han Li waves the papers aside, 'No comment.'

'We have proof here,' Nikki's face is flushed, her

mouth set in a determined grimace, 'You can do better than no comment, Mr Li.'

Han Li turns away unmoved, muttering once again, 'No comment.'

'OK. We will have no choice but to report you to HMRC.'

'I'm good. HMRC won't find anything,' Han Li stretches back nonchalantly in his chair, arms clasped behind his neck.

Nikki ends the interview.

Sir Timothy Robinson, the CEO of Metro University, strides confidently into the interview room with his lawyer, Sir John Piggott.

Nikki establishes her authority, 'Sir Robinson, are you aware why you are here?'

John Piggott, the lawyer interrupts, 'That's precisely what Sir Robinson wishes to learn.'

'We know about the finances of Metro University,' John replies.

'What has that got to do with the police and Sir Robinson?' Piggott fumes.

'There has been an unusual pattern of money

transfers across the university's accounts.'

'In that case, you should have called the finance director and not Sir Robinson who is an extremely busy person,' Piggott snaps.

'Mr Om Gulati has been found dead after an apparent accident,' John adds ominously.

Timothy Robinson, a fit looking 60 year old, knighted for his banking and philanthropy, looks at Nikki and John with a blank expression on his face.

'Care to add something to the discussion Sir Robinson?' Nikki asks with a half-smile.

Robinson, mouth dry, heartbeat racing, barely manages to whisper, 'I don't deal with accounts, Om does it.'

John pounces, 'You have no dealings at all?'

'No.' Robinson rubs the back of his neck.

Nikki switches to a charm offensive to alter the tone of the interview. 'Is the university in some kind of trouble, Sir Robinson?'

'Every university in the country is in trouble inspector,' Piggott interrupts.

'I'm asking specifically about Metro University. I'm not interested in the rest of the country,' Nikki answers tersely.

Robinson sighs, 'Yes, we had problems last year with the student enrolment. Our numbers were down and we were facing financial ruin.'

'How did you make it work?' John asks.

'My wife is a financial consultant,' he shifts awkwardly in the chair and continues, 'She found investors who could keep a positive bank balance.'

'You didn't ask any questions?' probes John.

'No. I didn't,' Robinson stutters.

'Has she got access to your accounts?' Nikki asks.

'No.'

'Does she know the password?' John asks.

'I don't know.'

'Did you tell her?'

'I can't remember,' all the blood drains from his face and Robinson's heart thuds hard.

'Can we have your wife's phone number please, Sir Robinson?' Nikki asks.

Nikki, Ayesha and John assemble in the computer room.

Nikki looks at Ayesha, 'Did you find any proof of Sir Robinson accessing the accounts?'

'No. Sir Robinson has not accessed the accounts in the last nine months. Om Gulati was the person who was accessing the account along with another person.'

John snorts in derision, 'I bet Sir Robinson's wife is involved.'

'We can't trace the third person to the computer terminals in the university,' Ayesha observes.

'Could it be hacked?' Nikki asks.

'It's possible that someone introduced malware into the computer in the accounts section and this third person can access from anywhere in the world.'

'Let's visit Mrs Robinson,' Nikki grins at John.

John drives Nikki to Sir Robinson's house in the most affluent area of Edgbaston. They enter the property through electronically operated gates and John parks his car on the deep-set driveway.

'I wonder what they're paying for home insurance!'

'These posh houses have unsavoury neighbours-some tenants of the nearby high rise blocks are notorious for drug crimes and robbery. Any comparative insurance website will tell you that this post code is the burglary capital of Birmingham with 41 burglaries for every 1,000 home insurance quotes.'

'No wonder they have an elaborate security system and dogs in the house!'

A Filipino housemaid takes them to the tastefully decorated drawing room, which has oak flooring, ornate chandeliers and double-glazed French doors. Nikki admires the well-maintained south facing gardens.

Mrs Irina Robinson arrives and John is immediately hypnotised by her beauty. She is wearing light make up, her natural chestnut brown hair complements her gracefully arching eyebrows and black eyes. Enchanted by her appearance, John is reminded of an article he read recently suggesting that Ukrainian women are the most beautiful in the world because of genetic mixing over the centuries. These Slavic people have a mixture of Persian, Mongolian, Turkish, Polish and Lithuanian blood amongst others. He recalls that the writer also observed that Ukrainian women are feminine but not feminists.

'It's a beautiful day, why don't we sit in the conservatory?' Irina looks up through her thick, glossy lashes.

They walk into the conservatory that has an indoor swimming pool. Nikki observes clean tiles, towels laid out alongside sunscreen lotion and the smell of chlorine which reminds her of her childhood when Keisha, their nanny, used to take them to a swimming pool near their home.

Irina presses a bell to summon the Filipino maid, 'Rosario, find out what these people want to drink.'

John says, 'I'll have coffee, please.'

Nikki declines, 'I'm good, thanks. I don't want any.'

'What can I do for you? My husband is at a business meeting,' Irina pouts.

'We have a few questions for you,' John leans forward.

'How active are you in the daily affairs of the university?' Nikki asks.

'I don't get involved with university work,' Irina shrugs off their line of enquiry.

'Do you have any dealings with the accounts section?'

'None whatsoever.'

'Do you discuss financial matters with your husband?' John is still captivated by her good looks.

'No. I don't,' Irina's shrill denial echoes around the conservatory.

'Has he told you about the financial problems?' Nikki prods.

'I've already told you.' Irina's eyes flash with irritation and ill concealed anger. 'We don't discuss money matters. Now, if there are no further questions, I need to go.'

'Goodbye, madam,' Nikki shakes Irina's hand simultaneously cloning her phone.

As soon as they reach their car, Nikki announces, 'Right, John, we will follow Irina.'

They watch Irina leaving her drive and follow her to a five star hotel in Hagley Road.

'You check who she meets and take a picture of that person,' Nikki suggests.

'Sure, Guv,' John agrees.

Whilst waiting in the car, Nikki looks at the last phone call that Irina made. She triangulates the number and realises that the person is on the way to the hotel in Hagley Road.

On the tenth floor of the hotel, Irina is pacing and the person she called turns up.

'What was the hurry babe?' he gives her a hug.

'The police just came to see me.'

'You have nothing to hide,' he kisses her neck mumbling reassurances and she relaxes in his arms.

'Guv, I took the bloke's picture.'

Nikki snatches the phone only to see yet another facial mask, but with those unmistakable blue eyes!

'Let's put this photo through our recognition software and compare it with the suspect's mug shots.'

'Do you think we will find him?' John asks.

'No.'

Nikki's phone pings:

Please come home.

Mum is not well

She wants to see you

Delroy

The message is from Delroy, Keisha Belinfante's son. But Nikki has no time now for Keisha, her old nanny. She is on a mission to catch the killer.

46

Nikki arrives at Ayesha's desk in the shared workspace computer room. Ayesha is engrossed in viewing the array of computers connected to each other, electrical cords dangling off the edge of the desk.

She tries to draw Ayesha's attention by tapping her on the shoulder as her voice is drowned out by the chattering from other cubicles, phones ringing, printers shuttling out paper and file cabinet doors sliding shut.

Ayesha turns around, 'What's up Guv?'

'Any news on the photo, John gave you earlier?'

'He isn't in any of our mug shots. By tracking his phone we can see that he is currently at the Metro University.'

'OK. He works there. I'll speak to him.'

'Who, Guv?' John arrives in the office.

'The bloke who was with Irina at the hotel. He works at Metro University.'

'You hacked him as well?'

'Hello, Nina!' Ayesha laughs.

'Am I that transparent? Do I sound like Nina, the

psychologist, playing the "by the book card"?'

'Yes, John,' Ayesha chuckles, 'you seem to be coping well.'

'Why shouldn't I?'

'You lost Tina, remember?' Nikki reminds him.

'We were going through rough times,' John's brave front slips momentarily, 'I, I... realised she was not in love with me.'

'But you loved her,' Ayesha encourages him.

'I must move on. Catch the killer. Let's go Guv.'

Nikki and John arrive at the Metro University campus, a world populated only by teenagers milling about in groups of two or three, kitted out in obligatory headphones and rucksacks. Most of the students are uniformly dressed in jeans but the occasional Chinese student passes by wearing bright colours.

Nikki looks at the headshots of university staff on the wall and quickly identifies the man who met Irina.

Simon Marks - Senior Security Officer

Nikki asks the receptionist to page Simon Marks.

A tall, well built man with a slight limp introduces himself, 'Who are you? What can I do for you?'

They produce their warrant cards. Nikki comes straight to the point. 'Can we talk to you about Om Gulati and Mei Wang please?'

'Sure. I don't know Mei Wang, but I met Om Gulati a few times.'

'Did you have any concerns about Om Gulati?'

'No. Why should I? He was the finance director and I am only the security officer,' snaps Simon.

'Did you ever speak to him?' John asks.

'No. We've never spoken.'

Nikki's request to view the CCTV footage around Om Gulati's office is stonewalled.

'Our security system is being upgraded. The engineers erased the footage of last week,' Simon recalls.

'That's a shame. May I ask, what was your occupation before you took up this post?'

'Sure, I was in the army.'

'Did you tour Afghanistan?' John inquires.

'Everyone in the army would have done at least one tour of Afghanistan,' Simon says, puffing his chest out proudly.

Nikki asks, 'Can you come to the police station to look at the photos of two suspects to see if you can identify them?'

'Who are they?'

'They're ex-soldiers and we want to learn more about them,' John adds.

'Sure. Anything to help the police. I'll be there,' Simon agrees.

Nikki's phone pings:

> Mum's blood pressure high
> Admitted to hospital
> Visit her please
> Delroy

Nikki messages back:

> Sure, will check up on Aunty Keisha
>
> Hope she will be fine soon
>
> Nikki

47

Simon Marks arrives at the police station casually dressed in a corduroy jacket, jeans and a maroon tie. He enters the interview room and looks around at the plain, spartanly furnished room. The soundproof walls prompt him to wonder if that is to muffle the screams or to prevent annoying noise getting into the room!

Simon sits on a chair chained to the floor and notices a device for recording live interviews; he readies himself to give a convincing performance!

Nikki tells the team, 'He's wearing a latex face mask.'

'How can you be so sure, Guv?' John queries.

'I am,' turning to Ayesha, 'Find out more about him and, Nina, can you analyse his behaviour during the interview?'

Nikki and John start the interview.

'Have you been to a room like this before?'

'Never.'

'We appreciate you coming in at such short notice,' John says.

'We want to do a thorough interview today so that you need not come back again,' Nikki adds.

'Sure. Anything to help the police,' chewing his gum, Simon smiles.

'Can we offer you a cup of coffee?'

'Yeah, one sugar please.'

'We will read you your rights as we would in any investigation,' Nikki informs him.

'I understand. Go ahead,' removing his chewing gum, he sips his coffee.

'You're not under arrest. You can walk away at anytime,' John says.

'We're investigating the murders of two young women, Mei Wang and Tina Wyatt,' Nikki begins.

Simon nods.

'Can you identify these women?' John asks.

'I see Mei Wang who was studying medicine at Metro University, but I don't recognise who Tina Wyatt is,' reinserting his gum, Simon leans back, cool and collected in his chair.

'We want to learn who has committed these murders and bring the perpetrator to justice as swiftly as possible,' John smiles meaningfully, 'Whoever they might be.'

Simon calmly holds his gaze, 'I understand.'

'If you want to call your lawyer, please tell us.'

'Why do I need a lawyer?' Simon narrows his eyes, chewing his gum.

'It's just a courtesy statement we make in an interview,' Nikki answers.

'OK.'

'Can you cast a glance at this photo?'

'Yes, he looks like a soldier,' pointing at one of the photos.

'What about this man?'

'He looks like another one.'

'Do you have dealings with them?' John interrupts.

'No. I don't,' Simon answers with a fake smile.

'What was your rank in the army?' John prods.

'It's confidential.'

'We understand confidentiality. What could have happened to these soldiers?' Nikki asks.

'No idea. Looks like they were living rough.'

'Why should they kill innocent people?' Nikki asks.

'I don't get your drift,' Simon grunts.

'We need to ask you these questions because there is a link between you and three of the four killings,' Nikki straddles her chair.

'How so?'

'Mei Wang studied at Metro and two soldiers are dead.'

'Are you speculating that the soldiers killed these women?'

'Yes.'

'Don't forget Om Gulati,' John adds.

'What about him?'

'He worked at Metro University too.'

'Tell us about yourself,' John says.

'What do you want to know?'

'When did you start working at the university, what does your role involve and do you have any connections with these people?' Nikki's voice is low and harsh.

'I left the army and joined the university as a security officer two years ago, I mentioned this already,' chewing his gum, Simon continues, ' I don't recognise the soldiers or Tina.'

'And Om Gulati?' John demands.

'I came across him occasionally in the corridor.' Simon sneers.

'We found financial irregularities in the university accounts.' Nikki casts her net wider.

'That's news to me.'

'Didn't you come across any rumours?'

'No. I'm only the security officer for the campus, not the finance department,' chewing his gum lazily, Simon is unruffled.

'Did you hear anything about money laundering?' Nikki probes.

'No.'

'Do you associate with Han Li?'

'Everyone in the city knows Han Li,' Simon grins.

'Do you admit to having financial dealings with him?'

'No.'

'Did you undergo major surgery on your leg?'

Simon laces his fingers together, 'This is becoming personal, detective.'

'Just a simple question,' Nikki assures him.

'What's that got do with the inquiry?' Simon shrugs, 'I had surgery for a fracture and it has healed.'

He looks around and announces, 'Am I free to go?'

'Yes. You're free to go. One last question,' Nikki stands up, 'Do you know Colonel Hastings?'

Heat licks his skin, his pupils are dilated, but he retains his composure and replies firmly, 'No, I don't know who Colonel Hastings is!'

Nikki ends the interview.

As Simon brushes past Nikki and John on his way out, he attempts to clone their phones. Walking past Ayesha in the corridor he repeats his manoeuvre.

Nikki's phone is impenetrable.

Nikki assembles the team and starts by asking Nina, 'Well, what do you make of Simon?'

'He has the air of someone who does not believe he is about to get caught.'

'Did he fool us?' John asks.

'I'm impressed with the way he handled the questioning. I'm also intrigued by his body language which changes during the course of the interview,' Nina adds.

Nikki fast forwards the recording and stops at, 'Do you know Colonel Hastings?' and exclaims, 'Look at those eyes! He's Colonel Hastings!'

48

Nikki enters a famous coffee chain near to the police station. She stands in line at the long counter which is stacked with espresso and frothing machines, bean grinders, bottles of coffee flavourings and toppings. She looks at the display cabinet filled with breakfast muffins, sausage rolls, pastries and cookies. Junior lawyers from the neighbouring court are lined up ahead of Nikki, waiting for their breakfast order before they start the day's hard grind, a few sitting on the comfy leather chairs working on their laptops, sipping lattes.

As Nikki is mapping out in her head a cohesive story of the killings, she's distracted by the background noises of coffee beans whirling in a grinder, employees calling out orders, dishes clattering, murmurs, laughter and the thick whir of the frothing machine. She moves forward in the queue smelling the freshly brewed coffee and acrid burned ground beans. She orders an Americano and, as she leaves the shop with a warm cup in her hands, a sergeant from the station comes running towards her.

'Guv, we went to Om Gulati's house, spoke to his wife and searched his study.'

'And?'

'She knows nothing about the university or the

scandal. Her husband didn't talk about it.'

'Did you find anything in the house?' Nikki sips her coffee.

'No Guv.'

'OK. Dig deeper about him and his associates.' Nikki encourages him.

The team gather and Nikki starts, 'We need to chart the murders and motives behind them,' and looks for the pen. She writes

Victim	Murdered by	Motive	? Victim wants
Mei Wang	Sam Masterson	Silence her	Be rich
Tina Wyatt	Ezi-soldier	? Stop finding out scandal	Be famous journalist
Sam Masterson	? Lawyer	Silence him	? Wants to tell
Ezekial	Heroin OD	Silence him	Prevent telling
Om Gulati	Moped mugger	Silence him	Whistleblower

'What are we to conclude?' John asks.

'One person is orchestrating these murders to cover up the money laundering scandal to prevent the truth from coming out,' Nikki summarises.

'What about Mei Wang?'

'Mei was a greedy girl and it's possible the man with the face mask and blue eyes got her killed,' Nikki replies.

'Where does Simon Marks fit in?' Ayesha asks.

'We know he's a clever ex-army man, with a shady past,' Nikki spells out.

'Can we not trail him?' John inquires.

'Yup, we will do it,' Nikki rises from her chair.

'Where do we start?' John asks.

'We'll visit Julian Pettifer now,' Nikki asserts.

As Nikki and John are driving to Julian Pettifer's house, Nikki receives a call from the duty sergeant, 'Guv, there's been an incident at Julian Pettifer's house.'

'What do you mean?'

'A woman came out of Pettifer's house screaming, "Help! They stabbed my husband". '

'OK. We're two minutes away from his house.'

John turns on the police siren and they head to Pettifer's house in Bearwood at breakneck speed.

Nikki shows her badge as she runs inside the house. In the study, Julian Pettifer's wife is screaming, Julian is bleeding profusely from his neck. Nikki rushes over to apply pressure to the wound and then asks John to take over.

Grabbing a long handled kitchen knife, Nikki turns on the gas cooker, dabs the blade with leftover vodka and heats the metal.

She then applies the red-hot blade to the bleeding site, cauterising at two-second bursts.

The bleeding stops. Julian looks ashen, as he has lost a lot of blood.

Nikki lays him down and elevates his feet to maintain blood pressure.

The paramedics arrive moments later, but have trouble inserting an intravenous cannula. She takes over, finds a vein, inserts the cannula and runs a litre of crystalloid, and then the paramedic applies a facemask delivering oxygen.

Pettifer's blood pressure stabilises at 90 mm Hg and

the paramedics drive him to the local hospital.

Nikki and John look around Julian's house. They see signs of a forced entry through the double-glazed patio doors at the rear, but no visible footmarks.

The assailant had ransacked the children's room and the bedroom where Julian and his wife slept.

Julian's study had books pulled from the shelves, picture frames disturbed as if the intruder wanted to find something hidden, perhaps incriminating evidence.

John and Nikki leave a further detailed search to the SOCO team.

'Guv, is there anything you can't do?'

'What do you mean?'

'The way you saved Julian.'

'That's just basic training, John,' Nikki smiles.

'You're a real-life MacGyver, and I'm proud to be working with you,' John gushes.

He doesn't get a response. John tries again, 'Using a hot kitchen knife to stop the bleeding, that's quick thinking, Guv!'

Nikki didn't want to broadcast the fact that, like the fictional TV character MacGyver, she is multi-talented.

Proficient in ten languages, a qualified surgeon, an anaesthetist, with engineering skills and military training in bomb disposal, it's an impressive résumé. The only thing missing in Nikki's life was the ability to love someone.

49

John and Nikki arrive at the hospital. As they walk past the franchise shop, they are met by the aroma of coffee and the scent of flowers as they pass the food department. Staff scurry to their destinations along the long corridor. The whoosh of automatic doors between hospital wings, whir of beds being pushed by the hospital porters, patients walking with IV stands towards the smoking shed greet John, who is not used to hospitals.

Julian Pettifer is in the intensive care unit, a tube in his windpipe and a machine assist his breathing. The doctors are keeping him sedated until all his systems return to normal.

Anna, Julian's wife, keeps a vigil at her husband's bedside.

She rings her parents to take her children to their house in the village of Alvechurch, 11 miles south of Birmingham.

Nikki catches Anna drinking at the water fountain.

'Hi, I'm Nikki Barnes, the detective in charge of this incident.'

'You're the one who saved my husband's life,' Anna swallows hard, trying to control her emotions.

'Yes, I happened to be there,' Nikki feels

uncomfortable at the unlooked for praise, turns away and almost stumbles.

'Watch out! I may need to patch you up,' Anna attempts a feeble joke.

Nikki composes herself, 'Can I ask you a few questions?'

'Sure.'

'Does Julian talk about his work?'

'He's a secretive person. Investigative journalism is a cutthroat business. He wants to keep shtum.'

'He worked with Tina,' Nikki says.

Anna's paper cup crumples and water spills on her clothes. She keeps quiet.

'I'm sorry to ask about Tina,' Nikki says bowing her head.

Anna collects herself, 'Don't be. Julian and I discussed his fling during our break in Devon.'

'OK.'

'He knew it was a mistake and would never leave me and the kids,' Anna mutters.

'Did he talk to you about Metro University?'

'No.'

'Did he leave anything with you?'

'No.'

'Our officers have searched your house and couldn't find anything.'

'I'm sorry I can't be of help. Please find the person who wants to kill my husband,' Anna pleads.

'Is daddy going to be all right mummy?' a girl runs towards Anna.

'Yes, darling. Daddy will be fine,' Anna hugs the girl.

She looks up, 'This is Elle, my five year old daughter, who thinks she's 20!'

'Who are you? Do you work with my dad?' Elle asks Nikki.

'I don't work with your dad. I'm with the police,' Nikki replies.

'You will catch the man who hurt my daddy, right?' Elle holds Nikki's arm.

'Yes, Elle. I promise you.'

Nikki looks at the doll in Elle's arms and asks, 'What is your doll's name?'

'Eva. She talks and cries. I can feed her and change her nappies,' Elle chatters.

'I wish I had a doll like that when I was little,' Nikki says.

'You can hold her. I will give mummy a big hug,' chirps Elle.

Nikki notices something skilfully concealed in the pocket of the doll's dress, a USB!

'I must play with your doll one day, Elle,' Nikki smiles, deftly removing the USB before handing back the doll.

'Come home when daddy is better,' Elle says.

'Sure. Bye Anna, I'll tell you if I find something.'

'Bye Elle.'

50

The team assembles in the incident room. Nikki informs them of the attempt on Julian's life and that he has been put on a breathing machine and is sedated.

'Whom do you suspect?' Ayesha asks.

'Simon Marks is our chief suspect. He has a military background, the motive and works at the university,' Nikki says.

'But we have no proof, Guv,' says John.

'Ayesha, triangulate Simon Marks's phone during the attack on Julian Pettifer and also find out which places he visits most, other than his house.'

'Do you think he has another hideout?' John inquires.

'It's possible. We need to explore all avenues,' looking at Ayesha, 'Can you send me all the coordinates and movements Simon made in the last week and highlight the two locations which he visited the most?'

'Yes, Guv.'

'John, we need to talk.'

John follows Nikki into her office.

'I've tried to access the Ministry of Defence's database and failed.'

'That's a first. You failed with the MOD then?' John smiles.

'Need your help.'

'How?'

'I want you to speak to your mum and ask her to put pressure on the MOD brass.'

John rings his mother and returns, 'All clear. We can go any time.'

'We'll use my Ducati,' Nikki announces.

'OK. How am I going to fit on the seat, Guv?'

'You will squeeze on.'

'Why not my car?'

'Too many roadworks. We can get there faster on the bike.'

'Sure. I'm ready for the thrill of a lifetime riding a Ducati motorbike!'

Nikki and John start the journey on the M42 and then join the M40. They take just 2 hours and 15 minutes to reach Whitehall in London.

John recalls learning about the background of Whitehall when he attended Hendon Police academy. Whitehall is a road in the City of Westminster, Central London, which runs from Trafalgar Square to Parliament Square. The street is recognised as the centre of the government of the United Kingdom and is lined with numerous departments and ministries.

Nikki reduces speed as she rides along the short street to reach the MOD building. Further down the road, barricades prevent people from entering Downing Street, the residence of the British Prime Minister.

Nikki stops to admire the grand MOD building, once the residence of English Kings between 1530 and 1698 until much of the structure was destroyed by fire. Over the next three centuries the building saw several changes. In 1990 the main building was redeveloped using a private finance initiative. PFI was also widely used to construct other buildings for the NHS, prompting the editor of the British Medical Journal to denounce it as "PFI: Perfidious Financial Idiocy."

Nikki's musings are interrupted as she gets security clearance, parks her bike and walks with John towards the main reception. They pass thick concrete walls and vehicle ramps designed to thwart terrorist attacks.

After an initial briefing, Major Tony McMurray takes them to the army archives building.

Nikki asks the archivist to give her the records of Colonel Hastings.

51

Colonel Barnaby Hastings

Nikki opens the document only to find that it has been severely redacted. It has become common practice for the army to black out the personal information of soldiers, but in this case, a number of pages were missing from the colonel's file.

Nikki turns to John and whispers, 'Can you keep the archivist busy?'

'Why?'

'Do it!'

John engages the archivist, Sergeant Leo Russell, in conversation while Nikki moves away from the security camera.

She takes a picture of the document and forwards it to Ayesha to remove the redaction.

She reads the name of the colonel's superior; Brigadier Afan Davies, retired, now living in Tenby.

After thanking the archivist, Nikki asks John, 'Fancy going to Wales?'

'Sure, one day.'

'I'm going now. Would you like to come or go back by train to Birmingham?'

'Guv, I read somewhere, sitting on a bike with thin pointed ends for long periods can compress the pelvic floor muscles.' John retorts ruefully.

'I understand your worries, John, but I need to see this brigadier now,' Nikki counters.

'Am I bothered about my pelvic floor? No. Of course I'll come with you, Guv.'

'It will take us 4 hours to reach the brigadier's home in Tenby. I'll do my best to protect your reproductive gear!' she laughs.

Nikki and John ride out of London, join the M4 and in ninety minutes reach a service station outside Cardiff.

They grab a coffee and Nikki rings Ayesha.

'Did you remove the redaction?'

'You're a slave driver,' laughs Ayesha, 'I'm sending it now. Where are you?'

'On the way to Tenby.'

'Really?'

'Yes, as in South Wales,' John interrupts.

Nikki opens the edited file on Colonel Barnaby Hastings. It shows that he was born in Walsall, a suburb 10 miles outside Birmingham, gives his rank, the battalion he commanded and lists his tours of Iran and Afghanistan.

'Nothing here, John, let's go,' Nikki orders.

The engine roars as they resume their journey, pass Carmarthen, Abergwaun and admire the Pembrokeshire countryside described in Welsh on a road sign as "Gwlad Hud a Lledrith", the land of mystery and enchantment.

This prompts her to remember her nanny, Keisha, talking about castles in Pembrokeshire and the Neolithic tombs on St David's Head.

Keisha and her boyfriend, Glenroy, and son, Delroy, used to come to this part of Wales during summer holidays. She would recount stories of Cemaes Head walk, where they used to watch fulmars, cormorants and guillemots nesting on the highest cliffs of the national park.

Andrew, Nikki's brother, always had questions, 'What do these names mean?'

Keisha used to cuddle him and explain, 'Fulmars are grey and white seabirds related to albatrosses, cormorants are large water birds with long necks and guillemots are dark brown and white seabirds which only come to land to nest. A fleeting moment of guilt disturbs Nikki as she realises that she has not acted upon Delroy's texts. She makes a mental note to see Keisha soon.

Time passes quickly, Nikki's thoughts run wild as they speed along, admiring the beautiful scenery on the way to Tenby.

John is entranced by the fashionable terraced houses crowding the cliff tops around this historic medieval town.

They pass the 13th century St Mary's Church and the defensive medieval town walls.

Nikki stops in front of Tenby castle, which is little more than a 13th century ruin with crumbling walls and the remains of a tower and gateway.

After freshening up, Nikki and John ride to the property of Brigadier Afan Davies.

'Wow. What scenery to wake up to!' John exclaims.

Nikki looks at the panoramic views across the waves to Caldey Island and the picturesque harbour, and agrees, 'Great to have a place like this.'

The engine whines at a high pitch as they climb the hill and Nikki pulls over at the side of the cottage. It looks as if it were straight out of a fairy-tale. The brick and stonewalls are held in place with lime and sand, in which creepers had found a foothold. They push open the flaking brown painted gate at the entry to the property. Admiring the cottage garden of honeysuckle and vines, they follow the dirt path to the front door. Nikki lifts the brass doorknocker and raps loudly.

52

John raps at the door again.

A booming voice answers from inside, 'Hold your horses. I'm coming.'

It seems like an eternity to John, but a short while to Nikki, until a man in a wheelchair finally opens the door.

'Hello, who are you? What do you want?'

'Sir, we're the police. We want to talk to you about Colonel Hastings,' John says.

'I recognise no one by the name of Colonel Hastings,' snaps the man in the wheelchair.

'Brigadier Davies, I'm Major Nikki Barnes.'

'Why didn't you say so? You look different, major, in your civvies.'

'Sorry, sir. We came to see you on a police matter.'

'Come in.' Davies trundles along the hall in his electric wheelchair.

Nikki remembers Brigadier Davies as a tall, well-built, handsome Welshman. He has a musical accent, a pronounced rhythmic inflection with strong and weak stress on alternate syllables. Despite his soft lilting tone, his soldiers swiftly learned that he demanded unquestioning obedience from his soldiers.

'What about Colonel Hastings and why?' Davies quizzes.

'Sir, we can't go into operational details, but Colonel Hastings is a suspect in a few incidents in the Midlands,' Nikki answers.

'Where do you want me to start?'

'From the beginning, sir,' John interrupts.

'Who are you young man?'

'I'm Detective Constable John Williamson, sir.'

Davies scans John's face, 'You look familiar.'

'Just one of those faces, sir.'

'I recognise faces. You resemble someone I've met,' Davies smiles.

'Have you met Anne Williamson, our Home Secretary, Sir?' Nikki inquires.

'That's it. Mrs Williamson was in this region a week ago and someone introduced me to her.'

'I'm her son.'

Davies gives a nod of approval, 'I like her attitude and what she is doing for the country.'

'Can we come back to the colonel?' Nikki interrupts.

'Yes. I can use three letters to describe Colonel Hastings. LBC.'

'I don't understand, sir. LBC is an acronym for the London Broadcasting Corporation,' John looks puzzled.

'L stands for leader, B stands for brutal and C stands for caring, that is Colonel Hastings described in a nutshell.'

'Can we go into details?' Nikki requests.

'Colonel Barnaby Hastings, Barney as I used to call him, was a great leader and his soldiers would die for him. He believed in the rules of engagement, but the Taliban didn't play by them. Every few days an improvised explosive device injured or killed a soldier, or one of the battalion was gunned down by the Afghan soldier or policeman he was training.' Davies pauses.

John offers a glass of water to Davies who continues, 'The soldiers saw him as a confidant and could share with him their fears, rage, insecurity, doubts, or just talk about their loved ones back in the UK.'

'I saw a bit of Colonel Hastings during the conflict, sir,' Nikki adds.

'Yes, the soldiers could share anything with him without the fear of looking disloyal, weak or stupid. He was like a father figure to them.'

'I'm baffled by all the eulogy, sir,' John mutters.

Did you tell your colleague here that you operated on the colonel's leg?' Davies looks at Nikki.

'No.'

'The colonel was standing in for a patrol soldier who had become ill. Unfortunately the colonel's leg got trapped by an IED and was blown to pieces, but our Major Barnes looked after him,' Davies gushes.

'What did you do?' John looks at Nikki.

'I fixed his leg with an intramedullary nail, which went from his hip bone to the knee joint.'

'No wonder our suspect walks with a limp.'

'What's that? What do you mean, suspect?' Davies asks.

'It's nothing. John is thinking out loud,' Nikki swiftly quashes John's comment.

'Barney recovered after Major Barnes operated on him and came back to active duty like a true soldier.'

'That's a sign of a real leader,' John adds.

'After you left Sangin,' Davies looks at Nikki, 'Then B or Brutality started,' Davies clutches the blanket covering his legs.

'How?'

'The Taliban killed two of Barney's soldiers one night while they were on patrol duty.'

'What happened then?' John quizzes.

'Intelligence reports suggested that Taliban soldiers were taking shelter in the nearby village. Barney entered the village with thirty soldiers and demanded that the villagers hand them over.'

'Did they?'

'No, they didn't surrender. One of them, wearing a suicide vest, approached them with a white flag to signify he was surrendering, and then!' Nikki glimpses tears welling up in his eyes.

He wipes away his tears, 'The suicide bomber detonated the device and twenty-five soldiers died instantly.'

'How do you know this, sir?'

'They captured it on the helmet camera of one of the soldiers and also from a drone flying over the operation site.'

'What happened next?' Nikki asks.

'Barney murdered thirty Afghan villagers and planted Russian pistols at the scene to make it appear as though they had been killed by the Taliban.'

'Did he get away with it?'

'Yes and no.'

'Explain,' John asks.

'Barney asked his soldiers to take pictures of the dead Afghans with the pistols in their hands.'

He sighs and continues, 'The helmet camera and the drone flying over the operational site captured the episode and contradicted the claims made by Barney and five of his soldiers in later investigations.' Davies stops.

'Was this case investigated further?' John asks.

'Yes. The Royal Military Police investigated. They concluded that Colonel Barnaby had killed the innocent villagers. After a low-key court martial, they discharged five soldiers and Barney from the army,' Davies mumbles.

'It didn't end there, did it?' Nikki asks.

'No. Barney wanted compensation for the soldiers who died in the ambush.'

'I'm sure there are rules concerning compensation to the families of soldiers killed in action,' John comments.

'Yes, there are. Barney wanted more for the families of these dead soldiers,' Davies says.

'Why?'

'He felt responsible for them.'

'What happened then?' Nikki asks.

'Barney became angry with the bureaucracy. One day, while I was driving along with Major-General Wells in the Welsh countryside, a four-wheel drive car came from behind and rammed into us.'

'What happened, was anyone injured?' Nikki asks.

'Barney caused the accident which killed the Major-General and left me paralysed since then.'

'How can you be so confident that it was him and why?' John asks.

'Major-General Wells commissioned Barney's court martial and discharge from the army which I supported,' Davies wipes his forehead and continues, 'He came up to my crashed car and shouted, 'Tell no one or I will kill your family too,' and drove off.

Nikki looks at Brigadier Davies who has lived through the trauma of being paralysed, 'Do you want us to come back, Sir?'

'I will make coffee and I will tell you his next attribute, C, which stands for caring,' Davies mutters.

'Tell us about his caring abilities,' Nikki requests.

'The court martial was a closed affair and the ministry didn't want to make it public that the soldiers killed innocent Afghan villagers. They gave Barney a golden handshake, with a paltry £10,000 each to the five soldiers who were with him.'

'But they killed no one,' John says.

'They didn't stop it either. In the eyes of the law they conspired with Barney.'

'What happened then?'

'They gave Barney a new identity and told him to keep a low profile and that the military would not take any further action.'

'Has he kept quiet?'

'I thought he had, until you walked in. He set up a fund for the families of the dead soldiers with the money he received from the ministry,' Davies relates.

'Do you know his new identity?'

'Yes.'

'What's his name?'

'Simon Marks!'

'Guv, you were right all along. You said it was the colonel.'

'What else can you tell us about the colonel?' Nikki asks.

'His mother, Ethel Hastings, lives in Shrewsbury. She may tell you more about him.'

'Thank you for your help, sir,' Nikki salutes.

'Catch him. Hope he gets punished, Nikki,' Davies responds.

Nikki messages Ayesha:

> "Find out where Ethel Hastings lives in
> Shrewsbury."

'How are your pelvic floor muscles, John?' Nikki asks.

'Recovered, Guv,' John replies.

'Hope so. We have a 140 mile journey to Shrewsbury!'

53

The tyres scream on Nikki's Ducati as she races her bike towards Shrewsbury.

They ride along the M4 motorway, cross the River Towy and enter Llandeilo, a town in Wales named after a 6th century Celtic saint.

John nudges Nikki, she stops.

'Guv, look at that bridge,' John gushes.

'Why don't you Google it?'

'This is Llandeilo Bridge, built in 1848 and is one of the rare surviving lattice truss bridges,' John volunteers.

'What's a lattice truss bridge?'

'It uses a large number of small and spaced diagonal shaped pieces of planks to form a lattice.'

'Shall we go?'

'Yes.'

They enter the Brecon Beacons National Park, an area of bare, grassy moorland and hills grazed by Welsh mountain ponies and sheep.

She stops the bike and turns to John, 'we can't go deep into the park. UK Special Forces use it for special training.'

'Have you trained here?'

'Yes.'

'What was it like?'

'I took part in a demanding selection exercise programme including the "fan dance".'

'What, you danced with a fan?'

'No. They also call it "Exercise High Walk", a 15-mile load bearing march, which takes place at the end of the first week of the selection course.'

'Did you complete it?'

'Yes. They use it as a guide to check if a candidate has the physical and mental aptitude to complete the selection process.'

'Did you pass with flying colours?'

'Let's say, I passed, time to move on.'

They arrive at a Sunshine Care Home in Uffington, a short distance from Shrewsbury town.

John notices a group of women sitting on the lawn with their carers talking amongst themselves in the vast grounds of the listed building.

John remembers visiting his grandmother in a nursing home which had similar decor, a homely common area with couches for family members and residents, wide hallways which allowed wheelchair access, a special events board, handrails along each wall, cabinets holding antique plates and silk flower arrangements.

A health care assistant walks past him pushing a drinks and snacks cart and a physiotherapist helps a lady to walk using crutches.

The receptionist calls the Matron who is persuaded to allow Nikki and John to see Ethel Hastings.

They enter a spacious well-lit room furnished with personal possessions. Next to the bed is a phone, a water glass, hand cream, and a framed picture of the colonel and a woman.

The sound of a toilet being flushed and a door opening marks the entrance of Ethel Hastings.

Ethel looks nothing like the lady in the photo frame. She's thin with an oxygen cannula stuck in her nostrils, making an occasional noise when the tip of the cannula moves.

The nursing assistant helps Ethel get out of her wheelchair and sit on the bed.

'Who are you? Why are you here?' Ethel demands.

'I'm Nikki and this is John. We work with your son,' Nikki replies.

'In the army or at the university?'

'In the army. I fixed your son's leg,' Nikki offers.

'Oh, yes. Barnaby mentioned an Anglo-Indian woman working on him.'

'Yes. That's me. We were attending a conference nearby and thought of coming to see you,' Nikki lies.

'That's nice of you. But why?' Ethel's eyes grow wide.

'It's always nice to know more about your colleagues.'

'Yes. When I used to work as a medical secretary, we had many people who kept in contact,' she puffs, easing herself further up the bed.

'Tell us about Colonel Hastings.'

John admires Nikki's acting skills, if he could, he would have nominated her for an Oscar.

'I named my little boy Barnaby after St Barnabas, a missionary and companion of St. Paul.'

'Did you always call him Barnaby?'

'No. I used to call him Abe,' Ethel replies with a toothy grin.

'What about his childhood?'

'His father left me when Abe was just a one year old. I met Frank, a policeman.'

'How did Abe, or Barnaby, get on with Frank?' John chips in.

Lips quivering, Ethel admits, 'I found out Frank used to beat Abe and didn't offer him any love or support.'

'What did you?' Nikki questions.

'What could I do? I was helpless. Frank also used to beat me up.'

'Did you try to help Abe?'

'I didn't have to. Social Services found out that Abe was being mistreated. They put him in a foster home.'

'Did Frank abuse Abe?'

'Yes.'

'How did Abe do in the foster home?'

'Not the foster home. He stayed in several foster homes.'

'Was he a trouble maker?' John asks.

'He started as a shy kid, but he moved from one foster home to another because he couldn't communicate with others, he used to soil himself and fight with other kids.'

'How did he change?' Nikki asks.

'Something clicked in Abe when he got counselling therapy from mental health workers. He began to attend school regularly, got good grades and wanted to become rich and powerful.'

'Why join the army?' John asks.

'His grades weren't good enough to attend university, so he looked at a career in the army,' Ethel replies.

'Did his mood pick up after joining the army?' Nikki asks.

'Yes. As he cared for everyone, he became the darling of the forces and got promotions,' breathing quickly, Ethel answers.

'Catch your breath. No rush,' reassures Nikki.

Ethel sips some water, 'You're kind. I will tell Abe about you.'

'How often does Abe speak to you?' John inquires.

'Every third day. He called this morning,' Ethel volunteers.

'How did he sound?' Nikki asks.

'Come to think of it, he sounded flustered.'

'How?'

'He said, mum things are happening. I need to concentrate. I'll call you as soon as I can,' Ethel begins to wheeze.

'If I ask you to summarise, would you describe Barnaby as bitter, power hungry?' Nikki probes.

'Yes, bitter. He's never forgiven Frank who died a few years ago. Power hungry, maybe. He grew up with no money, so he wanted money and to be loved.'

'Thank you, Mrs Hastings,' Nikki finishes.

'Guv, I'll pretend to be Nina Kowalski,' John chuckles as they are leaving the nursing home.

'You will tell me that my behaviour is unethical,' Nikki replies.

'Yes. You should've told the woman that we're police officers.'

'And get nothing out of her?' Nikki argues.

'I feel bad,' John persists.

'I told a half-truth. I worked with Barnaby and it was good enough for me to ask her questions,' Nikki explains.

'Can't argue with that, Guv.'

54

Nikki and John arrive at the station around 6:00 p.m. just as the domestic staff arrives to begin tidying up the offices.

Ayesha greets John and Nikki, 'You two need to freshen up and then we can discuss developments.'

'Let's gather the team together. No time for getting cleaned up, but we can have a cup of coffee,' Nikki says.

The team assembles and Nikki spells out the discussions they had with the brigadier and the colonel's mother.

'You were right to suspect Simon,' Nina says.

'We have to answer these questions: Where, When, Who, How, What and Why?' Nikki adds.

John sips his coffee, 'we know the where, when, who and how the killings took place.'

'Yes. We can pin the murders of the two soldiers and Om Gulati on Simon Marks, alias Colonel Barnaby Hastings, but we have no evidence to prove it,' Ayesha summarises.

'We have no evidence concerning who made the attempt on the life of Julian Pettifer,' Nina Kowalski adds.

Let's see what Julian Pettifer's USB tells us and see if we can come to some conclusions,' Nikki looks at Ayesha.

' First, here's an interesting piece of information before we look at the USB, Guv!' Ayesha teases.

'What?'

'Our detectives questioned Irina Robinson. She admits that Simon Marks is her lover.'

'We were right to follow her,' John adds.

'Wait for the explosion! Om Gulati recorded a video, let's watch it,' Ayesha says.

The video begins with Metro University in the background and focusses on Om Gulati.

'Hello, I am Om Gulati, the finance director of Metro University. This place could have become bankrupt as it has made huge losses over the past two years.'

He pauses, 'Simon Marks worked as our security officer during this time. Over a coffee, I told him of our financial crisis. He said that he had a plan.'

'I heard from him a week later. He told me that money would be deposited in the university's account.'

'I asked him about the source of this finance. He told me straight - drugs money- and challenged me to join the operation. He described how the drugs entered the country from Afghanistan via Europe, then Han Li, the Chinese businessman, takes over the distribution.'

Om sobs and continues, 'It was sinking in; this could be the solution I'd been desperate to find. I had problems of my own. My father was waiting for heart bypass surgery. My mother was pressurising me to pay for the operation in a private hospital.'

Om tries to compose himself, drinks from a can and continues, 'Steady income, working at the university, I jumped on the bandwagon of money laundering. I became bold and enrolled my two children in private schools. Things were going well.'

The recording stops and restarts, 'Sorry. All these emotions. My father's surgery didn't go according to plan, he developed complications. He needed intensive care which meant more money.'

Om shrinks back in the chair and rattles on, 'I asked for a top up. Simon told me that he would flood the market with heroin from Afghanistan and cheap fentanyl from Europe which would improve our finances.'

'I asked Simon why he needed money. He didn't answer, so I hacked into his accounts. I discovered that he transferred the money from the university accounts to two offshore accounts in the Cayman Islands, a loan to a company in the Channel Islands and also generated payments of false invoices to Metro University.'

He continues, 'One offshore account was called "Longlive Charity" which Simon operates. Han Li owns the other companies.'

Om groans, 'This was the biggest blunder of my life. My father died of surgical complications, my children are not doing well in school and, low and behold, my wife has developed breast cancer. This must be karma for all the bad things I have done.'

Om blubbers, 'I wanted to get out. I told Simon and he became angry. He asked me who else knew about my activities.'

Om disappears while he projects screenshots of various accounts onto the screen. When he reappears, Om pleads, 'Julian, please investigate this and put an end to the bad things happening. I'll tell my wife about my involvement and hand myself over to the police.'

The recording ends.

'Now we know why,' John begins.

'Yes. I looked at Simon's accounts and it shows only his salary deposited and,' Ayesha pauses.

'And?' John asks.

'The outgoings are to a storage site in Bournville and money to Sunshine Care Homes. He spends the rest on daily essentials.'

'Any savings?' Nikki asks.

'Only £745 in his current account.'

'It means Simon has no money for himself,' Nikki remarks. 'Ayesha, find out about the Longlive Charity.'

John asks Nina, 'What do you make of all this?'

'A few days ago I assessed Simon when he came for the interview. I can add a few more points. He continues to suffer from posttraumatic stress disorder as a result of child abuse and the later killings of his soldiers. He feels guilty, but he's resilient and is able to cope well and has an overwhelming need to help others.'

'What about these killings?'

'These are not senseless killings. He has a logic, even if we can't see it.'

'Should we condone these killings?'

'No. This doesn't absolve him of the crimes he has committed,' Nina concludes.

The meeting finishes and Ayesha catches Nikki's eye.

'What now?' Nikki inquires.

'Simon is moving. His car is on the way to Julian Pettifer's hospital.'

'OK. Make sure the officer on duty who is guarding Julian, requests the nurses to move him to another room,' she looks at John, 'You go to the hospital and make sure he is safe.'

'Do you think he will kill Julian?' Ayesha asks.

'Yes.'

'Where are you going?'

'To visit Simon's storage in Bournville.'

'Can I do something?'

'Yes. Message me the Wi- Fi code for his security system at the storage.'

55

John arrives at the hospital and, as he walks through the dilapidated corridors, he realises that it is nothing like the private hospital he was used to while growing up. He looks at the long hallway, so narrow that if a trolley or wheelchair came the other way, he would have to dip into a side room to let it go by. The walls, once smartly painted, now look grim as the cream flaking paint marks the passage of time. It's peak visiting time and people are entering or leaving after seeing their loved ones. He listens to voices, muffled or angry, and some sobbing. The air felt stagnant as if he had gone into a pit.

John enters the Intensive Care Unit reception and asks about Julian Pettifer. They had not moved him yet because of a shortage of porters. Frustrated by the delay, he muses that this is yet another outcome of inadequate funding of the health care system. Mr August Marshall, the health secretary, a close friend of his mother, would vehemently deny the effects of the budget cuts at the coalface. He always shouted at the top of his voice at the dispatch box in parliament, insisting that the health service receives a larger share of the budget than that allocated by the previous administration, which slashed funding!

The central nursing station looks busy with nurses gathered around monitors. A junior doctor chatting up a student nurse, a senior sister shouting at a nurse to have her coffee break. A cacophony of monitors beeping away at different rhythms.

Suddenly, the shrill scream of the hospital alarm eclipses all other sounds.

The senior nurse shouts, 'Find out where the fire is and we'll make our next move.'

The alarm keeps ringing and the junior nurse says, 'Sister, someone must have burnt their toast. It's coming from the sluice in a nearby ward.'

John observes a tall man dressed in surgical scrubs ahead of him, walking towards Julian Pettifer's side room. The man picks up his pace, enters the room and reads the charts kept at the foot of the patient's bed and approaches Julian.

John runs to the door and spots the tall man injecting something into the intravenous fluid bag running into Julian's vein.

He shouts, ' Stop! What are you doing? Are you the doctor? Where's the nurse?'

The tall man looks up. It's those blue eyes!

'Simon, Colonel, stop!'

Simon completes the injection and turns to John who leaps across the room and tries to grab him. John stumbles, topples the drip stand and the syringe pump alarm goes off.

In a daze, John sees the colonel walking towards him with the syringe.

He gets ready for a fight with his knees bent and turns his body in the confined space to face Simon.

As Simon lunges at John, he knocks over some steel pans, which clank, to the floor spilling their contents. John slips on the liquid, helpless on the floor.

A sharp object enters John's chest.

Simon has stabbed him with a needle.

John's breathing quickens.

As Simon turns to leave, John speed dials Nikki and gasps, 'Guv, Simon was here. Stabbed me with a needle in chest.'

Nikki, who is on her way to Simon's storage room, answers, 'Which side?'

'Right side.'

'Can you breathe?'

'Bit difficult.'

'Shout for a nurse. Shout pneumothorax, right side,' Nikki says.

John shouts and collapses.

Julian Pettifer's monitor shows a flat line trace. He is dead.

Simon has disappeared.

56

Nikki rides off from the police station to Simon's storage unit in Bournville. Being the peak of rush hour, speed limits had been imposed on the main roads. She passes the Country Girl pub, a magnet for medics to flock to after work, and recalls Michael Carruthers, a tall, handsome medical student, asking her for a date.

Not the time to think about it.

She passes Cadbury World in Bournville which she visited with her nanny, Keisha, and brother, Andrew, many years ago. Now Cadbury World attracts over 500,000 visitors each year, many of them children. She smiles as she recalls fond memories of their trip, learning about the history of chocolate and the art of making chocolate. Keisha explained how John Cadbury and his brother, George, sold tea, coffee and drinking chocolate, built up the business and developed the Bournville estate. The Bournville Trust, set up by George Cadbury, provided considerable philanthropic benefits such as schools, hospitals, public baths and reading rooms.

This prompts Nikki to remember Delroy's texts; she wonders how Keisha is doing and makes a mental note to visit her soon.

She arrives at Brum Self-Storage Unit. A security guard allows her in and, after Nikki describes Simon Marks, the guard directs her to Simon's unit.

A roll-up metal door secures the 6 x 6 metre unit with controlled access using keypad and fingerprint recognition. Nikki had gained fingerprints from Simon when he arrived for a formal interview. One less difficulty to overcome!

She accesses his Wi-Fi and rolls up the shutter.

The colonel's storage room reminds Nikki of her father - neat and dusted on the outside, any dirty secrets hidden away out of sight!

The room is clinical, military regalia line the shelf, photographs of the soldiers in his unit arranged on the wall, well-worn military and technical books rest in a pile next to the armchair.

His collection of books on money laundering and the Panama papers impress her.

She looks at a variety of head mannequins covered with silicone masks which, when put on, cover the head, neck and upper chest, with no visible joint line around the collar. They appear to be sculpted using high quality silicone.

No wonder Mei, Irina and others were fooled!

She finds Simon's laptop on the table with USB sticks lined up next to it.

She powers up the computer and types the password, "Sangin Specials".

No response.

"Afghanistan11%"

Nothing.

"25dead."

The screen wakes up.

57

Nikki focusses on the financial dealings of Simon alias Colonel Barnaby Hastings.

She opens the folder "Longlive Charity".

There are twenty-five names of women living in different parts of the country, each receiving £3,000 per month.

These are the widows of the soldiers who died in Sangin, Nikki recollects their names.

The account had a net value of £75 million.

A separate stocks and shares account for "Longlive Charity" contained £10 million.

Simon had provided for his dead comrades' families.

Nikki applauds.

A message pops up:

Edited your interview.

Here is the link.

Check. Suggest changes.

Will then upload.

Sgt Will Larkin

Nikki clicks on the link.

Colonel Barnaby Hastings, in full military regalia is taking part in an interview.

58

'I'm Will Larkin. In this interview, I'm going to ask Colonel Barnaby Hastings about his war experiences and where he stands.'

'Welcome, Colonel.'

The camera pans towards the colonel.

'Can you give us a little background about your personal life?'

'Born and brought up in this great city of Birmingham. Frank, my stepfather, abused me. I ran away and was fostered,' Colonel Hastings recounts.

'How did your stepfather abuse you?'

'You really want to know?'

'Not in gory details, but a summary.'

'My stepfather interfered with me and my mother found out.'

'Did she do anything?'

'She was helpless,' the colonel mutters.

'How was the foster home for you?'

'I struggled.'

'How did you get out?'

'I had a good child psychologist. He got me through,' he pauses, 'and, before you ask, no, he didn't abuse me.'

'Did it make you a tougher person?'

'Yes. I wanted to be strong, loved and powerful.'

'What about money?'

'Happy with what I earn.'

'How has the Afghanistan war been for you?'

'We should never have gone into Afghanistan. Look what happened to all the other invasions!'

'What do you mean?'

'Afghanistan's history is littered with occasions when foreign armies unsuccessfully attempted to invade; from Alexander the Great in 330 BC to more recent times when the three British invasions of 1839, 1878 and 1919 were all crushed.'

'The Russians arrived in 1979 and faced the Mujahedeen who were backed by the US and Pakistan. Russia, under Gorbachev, sensed the war in Afghanistan was a stalemate.'

'Yes. They left.'

'True. In 1985, the Soviets withdrew as the Mujahedeen, backed by the CIA's provision of Stinger missiles, had destroyed several Russian helicopters.'

'The Taliban had its role,' Will Larkin interjects.

'Yes. They helped Osama Bin Laden to build his base in Afghanistan.'

'In your eyes, are the Taliban the real bad guys?'

'A survey carried out in 2009 showed that half the Afghans thought the Taliban were more trustworthy than the government. They described the Taliban as a religious faction who attacked foreign forces, but not Afghans, and delivered quick justice.'

'Back to the point you raised,' Larkin interrupts.

'Which one?'

'We shouldn't have gone in.'

'They sent us to war without the manpower or the equipment to win it,' Colonel Hastings insists.

'Please elaborate.'

'We were short of helicopter cover, body armour and specialist vehicles to keep us safe.'

'Can you talk to us about your tragedy?'

'The Taliban killed two of my men. We discovered that the perpetrators were hiding in a neighbouring village.'

'Did you capture them?'

'No. A man with a suicide vest attacked us, consequently 25 of my great soldiers died for no reason,' the colonel's lips quiver as he completes his sentence.

'I gather you killed the villagers. Is that true?'

'If you say so,' the colonel grimaces.

'But you are looking after the families of the deceased soldiers,' Larkin pauses, 'why?'

'Because I'm a good leader and I care,' the colonel retorts.

'I discovered that the killings in Birmingham are your doing.'

'Maybe.'

'Why kill your own soldiers?'

'They were ready to squeal and put the operation in jeopardy.'

'Why kill the young female journalist and finance man?'

'The finance director wanted to come clean and the young missy wanted to be journalist of the year. Couldn't let that happen.'

'Are you a serial killer?'

'Loaded question.'

'What do you think?'

Colonel Hastings shouts, 'I'm not insane.'

'I'm not a psychologist.'

The colonel stares coldly at Larkin. I'm delivering justice which is impersonal and impartial.'

'In your eyes, is your act of killing justifiable retribution?'

'I'm not vindictive. I'm delivering justice, respecting virtue and honour,' he sighs.

'Are you trying to restore balance? If so for what?'

'I believe in fairness and equality. Not sure that I want to punish twenty-five families for a single mistake I made,' tears well up in his eyes.

'Do you assume all these killings were justifiable?'

'I regret these deaths. It's a means to an end,' he shakes his head and closes his eyes.

Nikki is overwhelmed by the confession.

She loads the footage onto her USB and cloud. Then she finds the phones and laptops belonging to the victims.

59

Nikki's phone pings.

'Hi, Ayesha.'

'It's me,' a man's voice answers.

'Where's Ayesha?' Nikki shouts.

'She's here.'

'Let me talk to her.'

'Later. You're interfering in my operation.'

'What operation? Drug smuggling, money laundering and killings,' Nikki screams.

'If you put it that way, yes. You messed it up.'

'I want to speak to Ayesha.'

'Who else knows what you picked up from my storage unit?'

'No one.'

'Did you upload evidence onto the cloud?'

'No, it's on a USB stick.'

'I don't believe you.'

'I'll prove it, Colonel.'

'Send me the user name and password of your cloud account.'

'Can't do that,' Nikki insists.

'You may have to lose someone then.'

'You can't do that.'

'Nothing to lose.'

'Give me two minutes. I'll send you the details.'

'Good.'

Nikki owns two cloud accounts. One of them contains encrypted details about her personal life and the colonel's footage. The other one has data from her police work, which looks genuine along with a copy of colonel's confession. She sends the details of the second account.

A few minutes later she gets a call.

'Did you say anything to John, your detective constable?'

'No.'

'He will be of no use to you,' the colonel laughs.

'I know you gave him pneumothorax.'

'Plain English, Major Barnes.'

'You punctured the lining of John's lung.'

'Oh, yes. It was neat. Pleased with injuring him rather than two killings in one sitting.'

'Did you kill Julian?'

'I hope so.'

'Can I see Ayesha now? Where are you?' Nikki pleads.

'You care, Major. I'm proud of you.'

'Like you, I too care, but don't go about killing people.'

'No. Just break people's bones and threaten them.'

Nikki realises that the colonel knows about her vigilante activities.

'I'm simply interested in seeing justice done.'

'You said it, Major, justice! Now, I want you to return the USB and everything you have on me, otherwise...'

'Otherwise what?'

'Your best friend dies.'

'No!'

'Good. So we understand each other.'

'Where shall I bring the USB?'

'I'll send you the location.'

'Is Ayesha with you?'

'Possibly. Come alone.'

'I will.'

Nikki receives a message:

> Nikki, mum wants to see you now.
>
> Please come.
>
> Delroy

She receives the coordinates from the colonel.

60

Nikki starts the engine and roars off to the Mail Box, a ten-minute ride from the storage unit in Bournville.

She parks her bike at the entrance to New Street station and walks towards a disused Royal Mail tunnel originally built to link the station with the Mail Box.

Using the torch on her phone, she can just make out the old light fixtures on the concrete walls, her footsteps echo as she makes her way along the passage. At the far end of the underpass, light streams down from the street.

No sign of the colonel.

Water runs down the walls in rivulets and drips from the ceiling. Nikki tries to avoid the puddles on the ground which makes walking tricky.

The underpass becomes narrow as she ducks under the structural pillars of the telecommunication company.

She realises that her journey to rescue Ayesha is taking a long time, as she picks her way along the tunnel she hears the sound of trains thundering overhead, the wind whistling and distant sirens.

Nikki stumbles on the uneven concrete floor and slips into a puddle of water.

A shadow emerges from behind and grabs Nikki by her throat and waist.

Nikki begins to choke, rams her elbow into the assailant's stomach and he loosens his grip.

She pulls away and stands in front of him.

A flash of light from a car passing overhead briefly illuminates the man's face.

'Finally, we meet properly, DI Barnes, or is it Major Barnes?' the colonel says.

'Where's Ayesha?'

'Let me finish the formalities. Thank you for fixing my leg in Afghanistan.'

'It's OK. You would've done the same for me.'

'That's the niceties over with, now I'm going to kill you and your friend, Ayesha,' the colonel roars.

'Where is she?'

'OK. Let me change tactics here. How many people know about me and my business?'

'No one.'

'Have you sent a copy of the USB to the office?'

'I didn't have time.'

'Good. Give me the USB.'

'Tell me, where's Ayesha?'

'USB first.'

Nikki retrieves the USB from her pocket and, in the process of handing it over, grabs the colonel's hand.

He kicks her in the stomach and face, followed by another kick to the head.

Nikki is lying on the floor, blood pouring from her mouth and nose.

As the colonel tries to grab the USB, Nikki catches his arm and gives a mighty yank.

The sound of a broken arm reverberates in the tunnel.

Nikki punches the colonel until he hits the ground and then takes out handcuffs.

Before she can cuff him, he jumps up, takes out a syringe, unsheathes it and lunges towards Nikki.

A struggle begins, as Nikki attempts to avoid the needle.

A sidekick breaks the colonel's jaw. He writhes in pain as she delivers another sidekick to his throat and he swallows fresh blood.

The colonel plunges the syringe into his thigh.

'What did you inject?' Nikki screams.

'You can't be a saviour again. You can't use Narcan to reverse my respiratory depression,' the colonel roars.

'Why?'

'The syringe contained fentanyl and curare.'

'Curare is a muscle relaxant. It will paralyse you.'

'That's the idea. One of us had to survive.'

'Where's Ayesha?'

'Do you really think I would tell you?'

Nikki squeezes his broken arm.

The colonel screams, 'You can't break me.'

'Please tell me,' Nikki begs.

'You made me lose everything. It's your turn to lose.'

'Please!'

'90 seconds gone, my muscles …are...weak!'

The colonel stops breathing.

Nikki calls for help and starts to search the tunnel.

A tall pylon with narrow steps catches her eye. At the top is Ayesha, tied up with tape across her mouth.

Nikki climbs up, releases Ayesha and they fall into each other's arms.

There are three messages on Nikki's phone. The last one reads:

Mum had a dense stroke

Please come

Delroy

61

Nikki's motorbike is parked at the hospital.

Delroy is holding his mother's hand while Nikki stands at the other side of the bed, gently stroking Keisha's limp hand.

As Keisha looks at Nikki, a tear trickles from the corner of her eye.

She closes her eyes for good.

Delroy gives Nikki a note written in Keisha's handwriting:

Sorry Nikki

I let you down

You have been manipulated

Speak to Glenroy Da'Costa

MEDICINE KILLS

2

A DI NIKKI BARNES THRILLER

Bakul Kumar

1

Nikki and Delroy, board the plane to meet Glenroy Da'Costa, in Montego Bay, Jamaica.

She wants to know:

How was she manipulated?

Who deceived her?

Why?

What can Glenroy tell her?

2

Ten days earlier -

Acting DCI Nikki Barnes solves the murders and closes the Colonel Barnaby Hastings case files.

The Crown Prosecution Service accepts the video recordings as admission of guilt of the murders.

Detective Constable John Williamson, stabbed by Colonel Hastings, is recovering in hospital. The tube inserted in his chest to expand the lung after the stabbing has done the trick.

The constant presence of Ayesha at John's bedside eases the pain of losing his fiancé, Tina Wyatt.

The National Money Laundering Agency takes over the investigation into Han Li's affairs. They decide not to investigate further into the LongLive charity. This allows a regular income to continue for the benefit of the families of the dead soldiers.

3

Nikki Barnes and Delroy hire a car at the Donald Sangster airport in Montego Bay.

Delroy takes the wheel, 'I'll take you on a pleasure trip.'

'I'm not in the mood after a long flight,' Nikki argues.

'Come on. We're here to enjoy ourselves.'

'No. We're here to scatter your mum's ashes and take Glenroy home.'

'I know that. Let me take you through the beautiful part of Montego Bay and get down to business later.'

'OK.'

The car drives past Sandals Inn on Sunset Boulevard and joins Kent Avenue.

'Look here no!' Delroy switches to Jamaican mode.

Nikki says, 'Who are you trying to impress with that Jamaican accent Del Boy?'

'I'll stop at Doctor's Cave Beach where mum used to take me when we came to Ja.'

'Ja, what?'

'Ja is a short form for Jamaica.'

'Got it.'

They drive past various hotel resorts from which western women, wearing the smallest possible bikinis, saunter onto the beach. The car stops at Doctor's Cave Beach.

Delroy yells, 'Paradise!'

Nikki looks at the broad swathe of clean, nearly white, sandy beach and turns to Delroy, 'All that fuss and only 200 metres long!'

'But, the beautiful trees and corals!'

'OK. Let's go!'

As they drive through the downtown area, Nikki observes the wide roads and cars overtaking at alarmingly high speeds. The old rundown buildings, closed shutters on several shops and children wearing backpacks walking along the street, bears a resemblance to the large West Indian community in Soho Road, Birmingham. Churches of various denominations at every street corner remind her of Keisha, her nanny, who held deeply religious views.

Nikki, accompanied by her mother, Madhuri, brother Andrew, and his boyfriend attended Keisha Belafonte's funeral at the Baptist Church in Small Heath.

Most of the funeral guests wore smart dark clothes, but some chose colourful dresses to celebrate Keisha's life. The men wore black suits, ties and smart shoes. No one was dressed in jeans, casual clothes or trainers.

They brought her into the chapel in a closed casket made of plain wood.

The Baptist minister gave a funeral sermon. Delroy had asked Nikki to deliver the eulogy at the service. She focussed her speech on Keisha's love for the people she cared about, God and how she lived out her faith.

Reading of scriptures followed and then a group of Keisha's friends danced around her casket accompanied by calypso music on steel drums, this was the highlight of the funeral.

It was a joyful farewell to a woman everyone loved.

They hear a bump. A car has run into the back of them.

Delroy gets out of the car to be greeted by a tall, thick set Jamaican.

He shouts in a heavy accent, 'Yuh lick if mi car.'

Nikki asks, 'What did he say?'

'He said, "you hit my car", obviously it's a scam.' Delroy turns around and retorts, 'No, YOU hit me from behind!'

'Yuh calling mi ah lia?'

'No. I'm not calling you a liar.'

'Yuh tourist damage if mi car. Want 5000 dollars to repair.'

' I won't pay. Let's call the cops.'

'Ha Ha. Nah Babylon here!'

Delroy looks at Nikki for help. She gets out of the car and the Jamaican's eyes light up.

'Yuh beauty!'

'If you say so,' Nikki flirts.

'Party wid mi an I figet damages.'

'Can we go now?' Nikki pleads.

'Mi fala yuh.'

'Why?'

'Pick yuh rah party.'

They arrive at Rosemount which lies on the outskirts of Montego Bay. A for sale sign welcomes them in the low-lit neighbourhood.

Delroy knocks on the door.

No reply.

After two knocks he looks at Nikki.

She removes a pen device from her pocket, fiddles and unlocks the door.

A man is lying face down, blood spreading out everywhere.

Nikki feels for his pulse.

No sign of life.

He is dead.

Delroy looks at the face of the dead man and shouts, 'He's not Glenroy!

ABOUT THE AUTHOR

I am a retired consultant anaesthetist, freelance journalist, blogger and a keen photographer.

I have published widely in peer-reviewed anaesthetic journals and authored three textbooks.

Amazon Author Central

Bakul Kumar Blog

Doctor's Mess

Author Bakul Kumar

Amazon.co.uk

ISBN-10: 1723479365

Reviews

A riveting read – Natasha G

WOW-what a journey to "Incredible India!"
Doctors' Mess - Bakul Kumar's first novel! Congratulations! A
reunion to mark 40 years since enrolling at the Medical school
in India, which reunites old friends from different parts of the
world. Afterwards a few doctors and their families embark on a
journey around historic Rajasthan! If you have ever visited
Rajasthan, New Delhi, Agra then you will certainly enjoy
reading this book immensely! This novel explores several
topics eg -(strengths and weaknesses of the tourists, their
relationships with each other and with their families back in UK,
USA and in India). Importantly, how they deal with their
prejudices is heartwarming too! It also highlights issues of
growing old, feeling lonely and unloved emotionally and
physically. It explores the complexities of their relationships
and their behaviour; their upbringing and their values. As a
reader I found myself totally absorbed in the beautiful
Rajasthan setting! I should add that this novel has love and
passion, adversity, loyalty and historical references, politics,
Artificial Intelligence and some medical terminology.
I highly recommend this novel! ENJOY the carry on ....

Printed in Great Britain
by Amazon